FULLER
MAN

Also by the author:

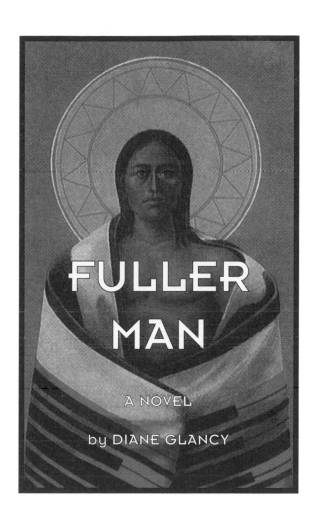

FULLER
MAN

A NOVEL

by DIANE GLANCY

MOYER BELL
Wakefield, Rhode Island & London

For Jennifer

Published by Moyer Bell

First Edition

LIBRARY OF CONGRESS
CATALOGING IN PUBLICATION DATA

Glancy, Diane
    Fuller man / Diane Glancy.
      p.   cm.
      ISBN 1-55921-271-3
      I. Title.
      PS3557.L294F85   1999
      813'.54—dc21   CIP
                          98-53782

Printed in the United States of America.
Distributed to the trade by Publishers Group West,
1700 Fourth Street, Berkeley, CA 94710
800-788-3123 (in California 510-528-1444).

. . they stood by the conduit of the upper pool,
which is in the highway of the fuller's field—

II Kings 18:17

And an highway shall be there,
and a way—

Isaiah 35:8

FULLER
MAN

Part 1

Hadley, Nealy, Gus

I dreamed there'd been other children, but mother ate them. Maybe they turned into fish or animals or birds before she did.

"Maybe berries," Gus said. Nealy chased him through the yard until mother yelled at us through the window. "Baby eater," Gus said when she couldn't hear.

Gus found a dead bird. He pulled out its feathers, saying the bible verses we had to learn in church. Nealy made wings from the feathers for our fingers. I stuck mine to my thumbs. Nealy used her little fingers because they were the lightest and her hands could fly easier. Gus tapcd his feathers to his middle finger just like you'd think a boy would.

July Fourth

You think I come to give peace?
I say, no, rather division.
Luke 12:51

Gus, my brother, came in late the night before. The house hardly settled when I heard Aunt Mary

Corder in her room. I listened to her prayers as the sun came up, watched the shine of light on the wide plank floor under the door between our rooms. I knew Aunt Mary prayed on her knees at an old chair by the north window. Other times, I heard her in the attic.

"Cold and snow come from the north," she said, "trial and sorrow. I always face the north." When Aunt Mary prayed, the house shook and the floors trembled. No one but Pastor Hill could pray like Aunt Mary.

Nealy, my sister, was asleep beside me. She had peace with God, slept in the crook of his staff. Never strayed. I turned my head toward her. Mother was on a cot at the foot of the bed, leaving the guest room for dad and his brother, my Uncle Farley Williges. My brother, Gus, was in there too.

We had come to Hammergies from Kansas City, Missouri, for the summer. Dad and Farley came from Kansas City for the Fourth. Aunt Mary kept them at guest's length, though she was a Christian. And I knew when she looked at me, I was in the guest room with them.

"Mother had been warned," Aunt Mary said. "The Williges family wasn't Christian." But mother

married him at the altar of Hammergies Church
before God and the wedding guests. The same church
where great-grandfather and great-grandmother
Corder had their children baptized when they came
from the Carolina Piedmont.

Aunt Mary prayed in a hush now. "The Lord
is a rock," I heard, "a fortress, our deliverer and
strength." But I couldn't call upon the Lord like
Aunt Mary. I stayed in bed after Nealy and mother
and the others were downstairs.

When I went down, Uncle Farley sat on a worn
stepstool in a corner of the kitchen. He propped his
elbow on his knee and held a bowl of oatmeal and
strawberries he had cooked himself. He had to be off
before the rest of us could gather for breakfast. Farley
was the photographer for the *Kansas City Chronicle*;
my dad was a reporter. Kansas City was forty miles
south of Hammergies. It was a city while Hammergies was nothing more than a country town, "where
our wagon had its shed," Farley said. He was after the
July Fourth in Hammergies. He sat like a bonfire in
Aunt Mary's kitchen. The wooden fan circled on the
ceiling like an awkward pelican.

Farley also would have stayed aloft from Aunt

Mary's soured disposition if he could, his cameras over his shoulder.

"Abraham didn't stagger at the promise of God," Aunt Mary said to Farley, "neither will I. Just mix your experiences with the word of God," but Farley was off before she finished.

Dad drank coffee in the dining room with his newspaper articles from last year's July Fourth in Hammergies. I tripped over the hook rug between the dining room and kitchen again. Farley turned and looked at me as he went out the door. "Want to come, Hadley?" He asked.

Our July Fourth was always carried in the *Kansas City Chronicle*—from the quiet country morning to the bonfire and fireworks at dusk. "The Hammergies Reune," Farley called it to the consternation of Aunt Mary—"the Sardine Bake, the Cornwallis." I had gone to it since I was born.

"Hadley hasn't had breakfast," mother said. "None of us has." Farley let the back screen slam. Aunt Mary's kitchen was like cowhide—pinto brown and creme, with her spatterware on the cupboard and chartruse print potholders on the wall.

"I want to go with Farley. Just give me toast." I

snapped at mother. "Farley!" I called out the door. He hesitated at the jeep. "I'm coming."

"You're not going!" Mother screamed.

"I am."

"Let her go," dad said from the dining room, and I knew she would turn on him when I was gone.

Farley drove toward the country. I looked at him a moment. I could be like Uncle Farley if I didn't hear the barb of Aunt Mary's prayers. After several blocks of stores which were closed for the Fourth, and some houses, we were in the country.

I wanted to talk to Farley as we passed the barns and hayfields. "I want to run like you, Farley," I would have said, but Farley was an artist with his cameras and I couldn't talk. He waited a while along the road with his pipe, watching the farmers at their chores before going to the Cornwallis. I saw the piles of uprooted windbreaks—the rows of trees between fields that kept the wind from the soil. They had been cleared for field-space and burned along the road.

"Now the wind can have the dirt again," Aunt Mary had said. "You depart from the faith, Hadley," she warned, "and you'll be just like the fields open to the elements."

I could feel the coming heat of the day as Farley drove to the covered bridge, not used any longer, but posted with an historical marker. "You take the bridge every year," I said. "It isn't even about Independence Day."

"It's the solemn morning before the revolution, the Civil War—any battle—" Farley said, "—even the Hammergies church supper on July Fourth. People's minds are transient, Hadley. No one remembers history," he answered.

I stood under the serape of covered bridge where the union cavalry had crossed the stream. "It echoes," I said.

"Hello there, Hadley," he called from the far end of the bridge.

"Hello down there, Farley Williges, Uncle Wiggley Williges," I called back. "I'm hungry, Farley," I told him.

"Wait," he answered.

I sneezed with hayfever, and felt my head begin to pound. But it wasn't time yet for hayfever. Farley knelt on the bank before a sag of rope across the creek. "Roof cover protected the timbers," I read the historical marker, "—skittish horses across the rushing stream. 1871." Over a hundred years ago. The surging prairie and torrents from the north. My headache consumed me and I went back to the jeep.

When Farley came, I felt sick to my stomach. "I remember the bridge picture," I said to him. I felt flushed with heat and the fear of another headache. The ones I had had since I was a child.

"We'll go on a short way," he said.

"I didn't take time to fix toast, Farley." I said. "I get sick when I don't eat. I think I have early hay-fever, and a headache."

In Polo, Missouri, he stopped and I got break-fast, though it was nearly lunch. My head pounded and Farley got some aspirin from the waitress. I jumped as he handed me the glass. There were boys in the street with firecrackers. The noise startled me as I ate.

"You really have one," he said.

"You know I get headaches, Farley."

He took the boys' pictures as I finished my milk at the table and we started back to Hammergies. Farley knew the country and towns we passed. We talked little as he studied the road. People took the *Chronicle* just for his pictures, Farley said.

"Do you feel better yet?" Farley asked.

"Not much," I said, fighting the bang in my

head. "Why do you stay at Aunt Mary's?" I asked after a while.

"For the feeling of family I guess, even ours. Miss Mary Corder keeps my pictures stirred," he said as the road rushed by the jeep.

"I wish she wasn't so much older than you, Farley," I said. "You could have married her like dad married her sister."

"Never," Farley said. "I'll leave Missionary Ridge to them."

"You're sensitive to the farm country—"

"You don't have to be from a place to know it, Hadley." He checked the cameras beside him on the seat and I hoped he would hurry back to Hammergies.

"Come to church with us this afternoon," I said, holding my hand to my forehead. "I go with them."

"No." Farley answered. "I heard Mary Corder shoveling coal in her room this morning."

"I told you, Farley—the farms from the church window—"

"No." He said curtly.

My stomach turned with the rises in the road and my head felt dizzy. My throat tightened in the occasional smell of smoke from the burning windbreaks and Farley's pipe—I knew I was going to be sick.

"Stop, Farley!" I said as my head swirled with the road beside the jeep.

Farley stopped and I barely reached the ditch when I got sick. My head pounded harder—I stood at the ditch for a moment, shaking.

"I want to go back to Aunt Mary's, Farley, I don't feel good."

"I can see that," he said.

Mother and Aunt Mary were in the kitchen when I came in the house. Gus left the ice cream freezer in the backyard and followed me in.

"I've got a headache," I said to mother. "I'm going to bed."

"But the supper—" mother said. I saw the baskets and jars on the cupboard—the chicken, green beans and Aunt Mary's biscuits. Nealy washed the strawberries.

"I've already eaten," I said.

"Where?" Aunt Mary demanded. "At Genny's?" She answered her own question. "I knew Genevieve would have her cafe open. And the burning of the windbreaks on the Fourth," Aunt Mary motioned to the window.

"Seems a fitting day," dad said.

"Would you stay out of what doesn't concern you?" Mother said to him. "Hadley, you disgust me."

"Mother, I'm sick." I yelled at her, and my head beat so hard I held to the wall. Gus stared at me and I felt my anger rise.

"Settle down, Ann," dad said to mother. Aunt Mary and Nealy were quiet. I knew they were probably praying like they always did.

"Leave me alone," mother started on dad.

I went upstairs to bed. I could hear them downstairs yelling. I remembered it since the crib. Soon Gus would bang his head on the wall, sweeping his arms as if against the hull of a ship. As if we were birds or animals closed up in the ark and it would be better to drown. Horse. Pelican. Hippopotamos. Giraffe. Milk-cow. Still they yelled and Gus swept his wings across the wallpaper until pictures and curtains fell.

Nealy came upstairs and knelt by the bed. I opened the sheet for her and we clung together under the cover sucking one another's hair until we could hear the silence of the flood.

I put my hands over my ears. "Pray for my headache, Nealy." I said.

She took a piece of my hair in her mouth. "You let your anger get away with you," Nealy answered. "Do you want an aspirin?" She asked as the chatham print of Aunt Mary's wallpaper darted above me.

"No, I just got sick."

Nealy prayed for my headache, and then for the family.

"He's our ship," she said. "Our mast and southerly wind. He leads us through the waters. He dries the land. He opens the mouth of headaches and gives them new tongues. Blessed be the Holy Gospel of our Lord Savior Jesus Christ Amen."

"Why do you keep praying?" I asked.

"Samuel prayed for Israel twenty years," Nealy said as she stroked my head. "He couldn't bring the ark of the covenant to Shiloh because of the people's distance from God. You've heard Pastor Hill's sermons, haven't you?"

"Don't bother me with that, Nealy."

I turned my face to the door that opened into Aunt Mary's fortress room. *From the north trials and sorrows come.* I felt the pillow wet from my tears as Nealy prayed and hummed.

I thought of the church supper, the foot races, and Pastor Hill's liberty sermon at the church.

I remembered the time I came back to Hammergies with Nealy when mother was sick. I thought about the setting sun, and how the bulky shadow of the car jumped from windbreak to field and back again with the dip and rise of the telephone wire between the poles. I felt the white frame Victorian house over me again that belonged to the Corders for three generations.

"I'm tired, Nealy," I said as I listened to the pulsing silence that followed the angry voices downstairs. I thought about the cottonwood and hackberry burning in the windbreaks—I thought about Samuel praying twenty years—I thought about Nealy's flute and the Old Hundred Psalm at Hammergies Church.

Heat invaded the room and the noise of the Lord. In the red haze of the setting sun, the beseiged town would rise in smoke. I felt its dark tides.

"But a highway will be there," Nealy said, "and a way."

A Long Trail

In the yard, Gus scraped his skin with the shaft-point of a feather.

"Don't do that, Gus," Nealy said. But he was becoming a blood brother to the birds.

Shame

Nealy and I stood on a corner of Hammergies by the feedstore where a group of kids laughed and talked. There was a cigarette still burning at the curb. Gus dared me to smoke it. I picked it up, looked at it a moment, "You do it, Nealy," I said.

She put it to her mouth, then threw it down. "It smells nasty," she said.

The kids laughed. Nealy stood unflinching before them, but Gus and I were cowards, shifting our feet uncomfortably as they laughed at our squeamishness.

"Aunt Mary will be waiting," I said, "with the receiving antenna on her head. Her telescope on the roof." I spoke with the bitter taste of pencils, the Ticonderogas dad used at the *Chronicle*. "Let's go."

"I'll take you," Jason said.

*　　*　　*

Aunt Mary had a frequency she kept tuned to us. She listened for radio signals from the angels. Sometimes in church she heard words from far away. I imagined Aunt Mary with her whip out there trying to rearrange the stars into Christian formations: Jonah's whale. Job's behemoth. Old Testament sheep. Goats. Rams. "How could we believe with heathen signs over us?" She asked. "Wasn't human nature enough to keep us off track? We had to have it overhead at night—?"

We rode with Jason, C.C., Horace and Clinter Krudup—Nealy, Gus and I. Horace with eyes close together as the headlights on Farley's jeep. Mother and Aunt Mary stowed away in Aunt Mary's house.

"We come shamed from Kansas City," mother tearfully told old friends who gathered at our return. Dad and Farley were the cause; "but she'd been warned," Aunt Mary consoled.

Jason's truck tore up the roads. I could hardly see for all the flying hair. Nealy screamed. Rain and clouds. Snowgeese flying south then north again, the strain of axle and wheel, of mother and father, their call, Farley's dulcimer and saw, backroads, drybarns and country.

"Jason, slow down—" Nealy beat on the back-window.

C.C., Nealy and I were in the truckbed, the four boys were in the truck, whooping over bumps while we yelled in the cloud of dust a buffalo herd could have stirred.

Nealy prayed for us. I cried. C.C. laughed, never did have sense to cry. But I felt the dustclouds and grit down my throat, the flying gravel and choking coughs. We screamed at Gus for mercy. "Mother is upset enough with dad and Farley. If we had a wreck she'd never recover, Gus." Soberness overcame the speed of our trip. Jason slowed his truck—mudflaps, coontail and radio gear. He had finished high school, like Gus. Nealy and I would return to Kansas City in the fall, if mother went back. Even if she didn't, Nealy and I could keep house for dad, Farley and Gus. My brother would be starting to the University of Kansas City, and driving the bookmobile for the city library.

Jason cut across a field to another road that went back toward Hammergies. We stopped at Flat Creek, and went wading, where we saw the car of Thomas Grostephan, whom Aunt Mary liked. He was with another girl that day. Jason and C.C. walked away with them for a while.

"Tell us about your pa," Horace said as we sat on the bank of the meandering creek. "Ma's dying to know why Mrs. Williges was crying in church again Sunday."

"It was shame, Krudup," Nealy said. "Shame. If Farley doesn't keep her weeping, dad does, and the paper and those damned calls." I so rarely heard Nealy curse I looked at her startled a moment.

"Tell us, tell us."

"It would seem dull to you, Clinter." Nealy said.

"Try and make it good."

> Simon Peter said unto them,
> I go fishing.
> They said unto him,
> we also go with you—
> *John 21:3*

Dad kept a dinghy in the backyard of our house in Kansas City. It was Uncle Farley's boat, but Farley lived in an apartment and the only place he had was for his jeep. Besides, dad used it as much as Farley. They fished Mussel Fork and Flat Creek while mother had the barbed irons and fish spears of her prayer meeting at our church in Kansas City praying for their souls. "*For, lo the day shall come when he will take you away with hooks. Amos 4:2.*" Mother read.

Nonetheless, Bill and Farley Williges traveled the lowland swamps, fished in the early morning fog knowing the women in Kansas City were on their knees. They would have divided Farley like quilt pieces.

"I'm going to be a fisherman also," Nealy would say from the backseat on our way to church and I giggled. Mother scowled from the frontseat. Gus also.

I wondered how it was when dad met her in Hammergies. I thought of her as a young girl, hiding in the mock-orange bush in the Corder yard that shed its white flowers in summer. Bill had been too long with Farley. He'd never been straightened. Besides, she smelled like the mock-orange bush and they were married. How long, I wondered, till she lost him—

"It was Farley that come between us," mother said tearfully. She couldn't abide Farley in her house, though he was there often for meals and during sessions about the paper. He smelled like stale pipe tobacco, was unkempt; had holes in his socks, which Nealy darned; was untamed.

The women prayed and Farley would come to church with us; then, as though remembering the fish he ate in Egypt, the cucumbers and leeks, he was off again to Mussel Fork. And dad went with him. There was a bond between the brothers that mother couldn't sever.

It seemed to me also that Farley was always at our house, or they were always gone for the newspaper. Stories happened any time. Sometimes the paper ran a section of Farley's photographs. He had been to the Pottawatomie Indian Reservation in Kansas where he took the stark land. He brought back a black, white and red striped Indian blanket which he gave to Aunt Mary in Hammergies.

"Heathen," she said, and threw it on the floor.

"I think July Fourth is Independence from the Indians," Gus told us. "We claimed their land more than we did the British."

"The Indian gave himself for us." Farley added.

I listened to them argue and thought of Jesus as far away as the Indians.

Mother preached at dad and Farley. When she threatened them, I left the room. I knew there would be other loud quarrels. Often, I knew, she didn't feel well.

Then there was the dinghy in the backyard that caught the flowers from her mock-orange bush while she hung clothes.

Yet it was Farley and dad that I liked. Farley had a Hudson we rode in for years. It looked like an army-tank by the curb. The Hudson could go anywhere until it met a lowland marsh on their way fishing where it remains. Afterward, Farley got a jeep.

> The Lord has prepared
> a great fish—
> *Jonah 1:17*

"It was about the time of the water trough story," Nealy said to the Krudups, "that mother got upset enough to come to Hammergies for the summer." We sat along Flat Creek as the boys listened to Nealy. "It was a farm along a ridge in Monroe County in northeast Missouri, where a water trough began filling by itself. Farley heard about it fishing. The farmer had always hauled water to the trough for his animals, unless a hard rain came along. But suddenly, the trough would fill and sometimes overflow, though his animals drank."

"No," Clinter said.

"The story was in the small town newspapers," Nealy went on, "and reached Kansas City through the *Chronicle*. Bill and Farley were off to cover the story for another week at the editor's nod— *'What was the* Chronicle *without them?'* Farley asked. Mother hated to be left alone, and spewed her usual threats. Even in the city, interest in the Monroe County miracle ran high. Farley's jeep took the ridge and his camera got the fence-splinters, the mule eehaws and trough water. Dad reported the feelings on Monroe County faces."

"The water trough story ran for weeks. Dad took us there one weekend," I told Horace and Clinter. Thomas Grostephan had come back then too. I remembered the cars parked along the road. *"'Spectators came from counties around, stood looking at it from different angles, scratched their heads,'* dad wrote, *'and walked away.'* Then we came back to Kansas City. And Farley, the only time I knew about then, slept with a woman who pursued him back to Kansas City. He hid at our house until she found where he was staying. Then the woman kept calling Farley."

"Mother nearly died of shame." Nealy said.

Gus watched her as he listened.

"So Bill and Farley Williges were back at their desks at the *Kansas City Chronicle* and mother's prayer meeting was back on its knees," I said. "*The Lord is my fortress and refuge*—even though he left her with Farley in the house."

"And the water trough?" Clinter asked.

"Someone got inside the fence the farmer had built around it, and kicked it over. The trough never filled again on its own." Gus said.

"But the fishgate stayed open for us," Nealy continued. "Mother couldn't forget the woman."

"Whenever she called Farley," I said, "mother raged. *'Get the suitcase!'* she finally ordered, and Hadley went to the attic for our grips. Gus had graduated and school was over for the summer. We left Gus's bookmobile job and our church in Kansas City for Hammergies and Aunt Mary's church here. 'Dad and Farley could starve,' mother said."

Nealy's Call

"Where've you been?" The chair scraped against the wooden floor as Nealy, Gus and I, came in the back door. Mother and Aunt Mary had eaten their supper and shared their sorrows. Iron sharpens iron. There was still the bitter taste of ore in the Hammergies water after all these years, and there wasn't anything left of the mines but the gray shed on the edge of town. Not even weeds had grown.

Hertess Grostephan had gone to the state legislature about strip mining.

"Nealy," mother began one of her tirades.

"Hush," Nealy answered.

We ate the meal at the table against their glares. Mother's anger flared now and then. Nealy could quiet her while I provoked.

After our dinner, Gus went upstairs. Nealy and I washed the dishes in Aunt Mary's hereford kitchen with its dark wood wainscoting and creme walls. Then we sat on the front porch as the sun went down.

Nealy was solitary at times. She looked off through the yard and wouldn't talk. "What's the matter with you?" I asked as she pushed the porch swing with her feet.

"I was just watching the sun, Hadley, and thinking about Clinter. I wanted to go out with him tonight when he asked me. I like to be with him, but I don't want that. I don't want that." She put her hand to her head, shaking her hair. "Pray with me, Hadley, that I will be strong." And silence consumed her again. We heard locust scraping their hind legs like chairs pushed back from the table.

"Nealy."

"What?"

"You're off again."

"I'm just thinking."

"About what?"

"I'm going to leave someday," Nealy said. "I feel it every time the sun goes down. Clinter'll ask me again to go with him. It'll get easier to say no. I feel the pull away from here, Hadley, away from Kansas City, even from America."

"Are you going to die?"

"No, Hadley, not that far. I think I'm going to be a missionary."

"That's like dying." I tried to protest. "Why

don't you finish school and marry someone like Clinter?"

"I'll finish school, but I won't marry."

"I'll take Clinter then."

"You can have him."

"It would be better than Horace."

Nealy laughed.

"You and I could have lunch together when we're old, go to the Kansas City Philharmonic. I'll write for the *Chronicle* and you can preach."

"How did you know I wanted to preach?"

"I didn't, Nealy, until now."

"Every time Clinter gets near me, I feel it rise, as a defense, I guess."

"Nealy, I need you," I cried on the front porch swing, but the Lord had judged between his cattle—Ezekiel 34:17, and it was as though she was gone already.

Sometimes We Played Church

Upstairs in our room, Gus whipped my dolls. Nealy made them tiny crowns of thorns. I hung them on the wall, pinned their arms outward like a cross. Nealy nailed their hands.

Hair Ball

"Hadley Wil-ligs," the teacher called my name the first day of class.

"Wil-lah-gus." I was at the last of the roll, waited for my name to be called.

I don't remember any teacher who could say my name the way it was, unless Gus Williges had been in class before me.

Nealy'd been sick for months. Throwing up. Stomach cramps.

Then one day—"Nealy wasn't on the bus," I said to Gus.

"She's in the hospital."

"What?"

"She threw up."

"I know, Gus—what else?"

"Dad called. The doctors found a hair-ball in her stomach."

Gus rocked back and forth in the front seat on the way to the hospital.

"Gus," Bill said, "sit still."

The doctors gave Nealy medicine to make the

hair-ball pass. When it didn't work, they gave her medicine to make her throw up. I heard her gagging in the room as we waited in the hall.

Then they pumped her stomach. Her eyes red and swollen afterwards and there were marks around her mouth.

Finally, Nealy had surgery. Mother stayed with her while Gus and I went to school.

I drew a nest of catfish whiskers on my paper. The doctors fishing in Nealy's stomach. Piercing her with their hook. They found the hair-ball in Nealy's stomach big as Farley's small camera.

Afterwards Nealy had to wear a cap.
But it was my hair she chewed on.
They never figured that.

Jesus

Under the covers, I had my hand on Nealy's scar. It felt like the backdoor screen where Bill fixed a rip with a thin, black wire.

Downstairs mother yelled at Bill. It was his fault Nealy ate hair. Gus wanted to be a bird. As they argued, Gus racked the venetian blinds with his hands.

Nealy took my hair in her mouth, but I pulled it out. I gave her my hand to suck, my fingers stiff as mud ridges along the bank of Flat Creek in summer.

Downstairs the house rattled. Took off. *Wooooo.* It rose. With Jesus the flyer. The head beam. Our Light. Wings. Feathers up his back. His name no man knew written on his thigh. Our high walk. Low flight.

"Nealy," I cried with her hair in my mouth, "we barely cleared the trees."

Hammergies

Whenever we felt a drought, we returned to Hammergies and the fields of Missouri. It was the beginning of my awareness. Nealy's soft lap when I lay down, the lines of corduroy on my face when I awoke. And there was Gus on the other side of Nealy. William, of course, was his name, but dad took the Gus from Williges and it stayed with him.

I saw the flight of birds overhead as we left. Some of them would follow us to Hammergies.

Nealy said we could know the angels like birds. We could leave seed and they'd eat. She'd put a dish for the angels outside our windowsill in winter. In the summer she said the angels could find their seed in the yard and hedges.

Gus was at the University of Kansas City now, and dad and Farley were traveling in Tennessee from their last call, covering farm droughts.

There also had been fierce droughts which I was not alive to remember. "Every twenty-two years one comes," Aunt Mary said. She had things in compartments like printer's drawers. Creek and wells dried up and the dryghost of old droughts haunted them. She translated worries from the dustrise of our race. She remembered to Adam our droughts and sins. She used the gospel as a rod.

"Hadley never could sit still," Aunt Mary said as I flinched in the pew. I had knocked the hymn book on the floor when we were seated in the church.

My memory made jumps and starts from Kansas City, Bucyrus, Bynumville, Boswell—down dirt roads in the July sun. I passed treestump fences, haystrawed fields, from the window of the church in Hammergies. Haystooks in the fields stood like gravestones in the cemetery outside the church where my ancestors were buried. Mother sometimes lamented them. Her words were cold, confining as fences and windbreaks. She divided between the ones who behaved themselves and those who didn't. She had compartments like Aunt Mary.

Windbreaks had burned in the fields around Hammergies. When the power of the gospel had gone, I kept the fundaments until they too, grew weary, and I was burning them. We stood in our usual place on the second row. Pastor Hill called upon Aunt Mary for prayer and the church opened with hallelujahs and her prayer to the Lord for our redemption; our Savior, unto him be power, majesty, dominion and might, now and forever. I stood un-moving as fences until I raged with the land in the smoke of all the burning fires of fields. I had returned to the cloak room when Aunt Mary finished praying.

Watching Him Paint the House Across the Street

I stayed in the cloak room one afternoon in grade school for the privilege of remaining apart. With umbrellas and coats upon their hooks, I stood like him against the ladder.

The Sermon

Hammergies Church was a cross, when you knew it was a cross, with a door at the foot, a pulpit at the head, a long row of pews up the center and side pews in the arms for mourners and late-comers where an old coal stove had been. I saw Hertess Grostephan and Winifred, her sister-in-law. I knew others, Aunt Mary's neighbors and friends. Thomas Grostephan sat with Clinter Krudup. C.C. and Jason sat in a side pew. I could see the white hat C.C. wore as I listened to Pastor Hill.

The bricks on the sidewalk up to the church were printed with Hammergies, the town where my ancestors came from the Carolina Piedmont where my grandmother was born, then Aunt Mary and mother. I thought of the feedstore in Hammergies, the barley sacks, nubby in the dust ridges of the sun. Coarse grainsacks pitted with uncharted roads we used to travel. Hammergies to Kansas City to Indiana long ago, and back to Kansas City when the *Chronicle* revived.

Aunt Mary said, "Amen," to Pastor Hill's sermon. She put her hand on mine and I listened again as he preached about the Philistine attack on Israel after the ark of the covenant was returned to them.

"Someday I'm going to know the Bible like Brother Hill," Nealy had said. But I heard the caterwauls of my heart as he preached.

The sermon left me cold, damp, retreated in the cave. I had a plot of lentils upon which drought and blizzard fell, and the iron feet of locusts. I felt my will—the beast in myself. I couldn't bow my knees. Mother had pinches, stiff looks and threats for my stubbornness, until I withdrew from her. It was Nealy I talked to. I was like mother, full of fears, unrest, resentment, discontent. I moved my hand from under Aunt Mary's.

Gus was always disgruntled too, but his was outward directed, while mine seethed within. Gus had been arrested at a political rally. I sat in church with my head miles away.

Plowing Up the Windbreaks

I tore against the divisions, the hurricane and hailstone, the fencepost, furrows, the windbreaks and straight roads.

"Nealy. Nealy." I could never catch her. She laughed on the hog's ear of land.

"Can't you behave, Hadley?" Aunt Mary and mother always said.

I would go to church. Then later, "Nealy, where is God? In church I believe, but when I am alone, I don't know."

Nealy played the flute. Uncle Farley the saw, like great-grandpa from the Carolina Piedmont.

"Not such pleasure," Aunt Mary said, "since mean Edgar Stevens rushed into the church revival after his wife and child, and was saved."

Now if Farley would come too, and dad. The wind wailed in the weather stripping of the door, played Farley with the dulcimer and saw. Aunt Mary sighed. But unknown to her, I, too, was far away as we went to bed that windy summer night.

Dad and Farley Were Gone Again

Mother mourned in Hammergies. She would return to Kansas City in the fall. It was her Christian duty. I was only waiting too. I couldn't fit into their printer's drawers. Whack. Whack. In the woodpile, chips flew. In the wind again. Chariots of iron. Fire into the plains. I trembled on my knees in the Hammergies Church. My neck stiffened. "I have a headache. I can't pray, Nealy. I want to leave." They let me up, but Nealy stayed.

"You'll go far away before you come back," Pastor Hill said.

I left anyway.

Graduation

"I'm tired," I said to Nealy as I put on my robe before commencement. "A moth kept me awake last night, then someone drove through our yard and got stuck."

Our friends laughed in the noisy corner of the room.

"It's the rain we've had."

Mother and dad, Gus, Aunt Mary and Farley, had gone to the auditorium. Nealy stayed behind.

"What am I going to do without you next year, Nealy?"

"What am I going to do without you?" She returned.

"Who was it anyway who ran across our yard?"
I asked.

"I don't know." We both had tears in our eyes.
"I saw the tracks in the yard this morning. So did
Bill."

"And mother," I added.

"Whoever it was—some of his friends must
have pulled him out."

"I'm surprised you slept through it, Nealy." I
said. "I also dreamed someone was in the house. I
must have heard other noises. But not enough to
wake me up. Later I dreamed Gus drove the bookmobile into the garage and it wouldn't fit, but he kept
driving and it lifted the ceiling."

A friend who heard me laughed at the bookmobile.

"The ceiling curled up. I still can see it."

"Are you going to the University of Kansas
City next year with Gus?" The friend asked in the
crowded waiting room.

"No, I'm going to the University of Missouri in
Columbia."

A teacher called our attention. Nealy kissed me
and left for the auditorium.

A friend handed me a note as I wiped my eyes.

"When you leave, knocking over chairs, making holes in the walls, I'll remember your swift grace."

"We could get everyone in the bookmobile." A friend whispered behind me when we were seated for commencement.

"The bookmobile's at the library."

"Come on, Hadley," a boy beside me repeated. "Gus has the keys. They're probably on his dresser."

I ignored him, and wondered why an important event passed without significance. Maybe it was the speaker who was boring us. Maybe it was the fierce lives we came from that diverted its significance. I knew students whose lives were overpowered by their parents' turbulence, by the state of the nation, by the sluggardly move of their hopes toward a red sky.

"I can't get the keys to the bookmobile."

"We'll just drive it around the block."

"No."

They were quiet for a while.

"Once around the block."

I whispered angrily. "We could get arrested. Gus would be fired."

We stood, and walked to the platform. I climbed the stairs behind the others. Aunt Mary, mother, Bill, Uncle Farley, Nealy and Gus were in the second row of the audience. I saw them when I first came in.

I would be without Nealy in the years ahead. I followed her, though I was older. She knew what to do and did it with conviction. I wasn't sure yet of anything.

The principal of the high school shook my hand. I felt the diploma thrust into my fist. I changed the tassel to the other side of my hat.

"If you mention the bookmobile one more time—"

I had gone to the house after graduation exercises. Uncle Farley took my picture. I opened Aunt Mary's gift and other presents. Then my friends came by for me. I wanted Nealy to go, but she wouldn't. Gus was supposed to turn in the keys to the garage at the library after his arrest, but he hadn't as yet. I picked up the keys as I left.

"Why'd you have to go home?"

"Aunt Mary had a present she wanted to give me."

"What was it?"

"You'll laugh—A Bible. And a trip to the Carolinas—where the Corders are from."

We sat in the car while the two who were already eighteen went into the store for beer.

"Give Hadley a bottle."

"I don't like to drink."

"This is graduation night. Let your wings droop."

"I'm not wearing wings. You can be obtuse."

"Listen to those college words."

We drove around the city, not doing anything. We hit a party, but stayed a short while. We drove farther.

I held up the keys.

"The bookmobile?"

"No, the keys to the garage."

"The bookmobile's in the parking lot."

"But the keys're in the garage."

The keys to the bookmobile were on a hook in the garage. The bookmobile was in the lot. It stared with a roar. We sat on the floor as a friend drove from the library lot, dropping over the curb as he turned onto the street. The bookmobile rocked like a heavy boat on the water. We went around the block, lurching back and forth against one another. My friend tried to floor the bookmobile at a stop light. We were laughing so hard. Books falling off the shelves. The world of knowledge and school toppling for a moment like the great walls of Jericho.

Carolina

Gus was the only one to get out of going to the Carolinas. I sat in the backseat between mother and Aunt Mary. Nealy was in front between dad and Farley. Gus had to drive the bookmobile without pay as part of his probation. He also had to go to the University of Kansas City for summer school.

We had postponed the trip until I finished my community service to the library, returning books to the shelves half the summer for taking the bookmobile from the lot on graduation night. Mother still refused to speak of it.

It had been Aunt Mary's idea for Nealy, mother and me to go by ourselves. But it was over a thousand miles from Kansas City to the Carolinas. Mother nor Aunt Mary could drive that far. Nealy and I were too young to have the experience for such a trip. Bill decided he would go and write a travel article. Farley would take pictures.

Perche. Houstonia. Auxvasse.

We were past St. Louis and into Illinois before Farley said anything. Rain came down like mock-orange petals. It was the first silence I remembered between dad and his brother.

"Anywhere you want to stop, Farley." Mother sensed the rift between them and used every opportunity to pound her wedge.

Farley passed a long line of cars and humped a railroad crossing when it was his turn to drive. Aunt Mary screamed. "Do that again, Farley—I'll trail you on a string."

We turned off the divided highway and traveled a backroad.

"Slow it down, Geronimo." Dad said to Farley.

We stayed the first night in Vincennes.

Indiana was a narrow state across the bottom. I thought of Hammergies and the drugstore and Thomas Grostephan when we started off the next morning. My imaginings passed like cars until mother's head nodded and Bill picked up speed.

We were into the hills of Kentucky by afternoon. Bill took notes as he drove. Mother worried that he would run off the road. Then she smelled something burning. "Was it the engine?" She was going west when we should have been going east— Farley looked at her coldly.

"Delaware. Maine. What were cars from other states doing on the road so far from where they belonged?" Mother thought out loud from time to time.

"Aren't we going through the mountains?" Nealy asked, reading the map for Bill.

"Not yet." He answered.

"I thought that arrow said the other way." I heard mother say.

"No, Ann. We're going the right way."

Farley took his finger and pointed to something on the map. Nealy smiled. He patted my knee from the frontseat. I smiled at him too.

Suddenly he hit his hand on the seat.

Aunt Mary jumped. "What's the matter, Farley?"

"I left my robe on the back of the bathroom door in the motel last night."

"Could we call and have them send it?"

"They rarely do." Farley said. "Drat. My new

robe. Bought it just for the trip to the stomping grounds. The old homestead."

"It isn't your family that's from the Carolinas." Aunt Mary exploded on him. "I don't expect it to be as interesting to you."

"It isn't." Farley was beginning to feel like himself.

I turned on the radio.

"Turn it down, Hadley, before your mother starts on one of her series." Dad told me.

Dad took notes when it was Farley's turn to drive. "Man behind his mule in tobacco field. House on stilts. White flowers scattered along the road like spilled milk." I read what he wrote.

"How do you write a travel article?" I asked him.

"Just by what I'm doing, Hadley." He answered. "Start small, with details, the bigger picture comes from them."

"All the Negroes," mother exclaimed. "What are they doing on the road?"

"Lexington. Clover Bottom. Climax." Bill wrote.

Farley took pictures when we stopped. Dad was

out talking to people on the street when we had dinner. We ate without him and Farley, then waited while they ordered.

"I don't think I can go a mile farther." Aunt Mary said. "I'm not used to trips. When can we stop for the night?"

"It was you and Ann that insisted on motel reservations every night." Farley informed Mary Corder. "Middlesboro can't be more than an hour or two away."

"Great heavens." She said. "You should have taken us into consideration when you made the reservations," mother told Bill.

"I didn't know it would be so much slower traveling with you and the girls," Bill explained. "Everyone has to go to the bathroom at different times—"

"Farley has to stand in the field."

"We gaged the day's travels from our past experience." Farley interjected. "Four hundred miles is not too far to go in a day."

"Unless we stop all the time," Ann suggested.

"And travel with two women who think the roads fold up at 6:00 p.m. and if they don't have a room, they will be out in the dark all night."

"Close it down, Farley." Bill warned.

                    *   *   *

We didn't see the train tracks outside the motel in Middlesboro. We didn't know they were there until we were in bed and the first train passed. Mother sat up. "Jesus!" She exclaimed. I turned to Nealy in bed and we giggled. I heard Bill's typewriter peck in their room when the train had passed. "Jesus," mother said again, and we giggled until the bed jumped.

The next day in Tennessee, Farley stopped to develop his film, and Bill called the newspaper office in Kansas City. I saw the pictures Farley developed. He took one of Bill at the motel window, looking into the darkness as the train passed. I held to Farley's arm a moment—the aloneness of my father at his typewriter came through as swift as the train in Middlesboro. Farley patted my hand.

"What's the use of all of it?" Mother asked when we were on the road.

Knoxville. Pine Grove. Gatlinburg.

"Well, it's our living, Ann."

"I thought pine trees were only in the north." I said.

"My dear," Aunt Mary replied. "We have more

pines in the south than they ever thought of in the north."

The Smoky Mountains stood before us in their rolling greenness. Nealy gasped. Farley's cameras clicked.

"All I can see is fog," mother said.

Traffic was slow in the mountains. My ears popped. I could see down into the valleys from the curved, mountain roads. I held to Farley's arm or Nealy's.

When we stopped in a rest area, the air was cool and quiet, though crowded with people.

"It's because your ears are stopped up with the altitude," Farley said. "Yawn until they pop and you can hear the birds."

I laughed.

Mother and Aunt Mary looked for the rest rooms. When they were gone, Nealy yodeled into the valley. Farley took her picture.

"I like the mountains, Nealy," I said.

We held hands as we looked down at the winding road far below. It was as though we became the pines, yearning for the other, sharing the crisp air we breathed. Farley watched the people. Dad sat in the car with some thought.

               *   *   *

"Wheeler, Woods, Adams, Siceloff, Corder," Aunt Mary reviewed the family history as we left Cherokee, North Carolina, the following morning and started toward Asheville. Aunt Mary was almost giddy with her thoughts. It had been years since she'd been back. Now that she was nearing the origins of our family, she was zealous as she was in church.

Nealy and I watched the highway, the gray sky, the low hills. We passed a slow truck on an ascent, but it passed us on a downward incline. We passed it once again as we climbed another hill, but soon, it went around us.

Mother was upset that traffic didn't always travel the same speed.

"Man on front porch getting hair cut." I said for Bill's notes.

"I saw it." He said.

"Don't you want a picture?" I asked Farley.

"No. That kind has a shot gun under his chair."

"Another thing you know from experience?" Mother asked.

We passed a backwoods yard sale. Clothes and junk.

"You need another robe?" Nealy asked Farley.

"And a few fleas to go with it?" I said.

"I'll keep driving." Farley smiled.

A small brook followed the backroad. I watched it for a while then dozed between conversations.

"The Piedmont area below the mountains," Aunt Mary's voice startled me. "Your great-grandmother always wanted to live in Winston-Salem, Hadley," she told me as I stared at her.

Mother didn't like what she saw. "Easterners and southerners should be aristocrats." She stated, though we were in the back-hill country.

"Makes sense." Farley said.

"Mother's sense." I thought. I wondered how the world must look to her. How did she get that way? Or rather, why didn't she grow out of that way.

At least, Bill stayed with her. He must be from good stock. But he and Farley never talked much about their family. Mother and Aunt Mary Corder took up all the room there was for that.

In Asheville, Aunt Mary rummaged through the remains of our family's heritage. The Corder lot she believed she found was a weedy vacant corner.

Farley took some shots of it, reveling in the irony.

The cemetery on the edge of the mountain town was weedy also. Aunt Mary sorted through the crumbling gravestones.

"Smile." Farley said with his camera.

She stood by a crumbling brick wall and a few leaning stones, talking all the time of Corder history and a few distant relatives we were going to find. But no one answered the few times she called.

Finally we drove by the house of a decrepit woman, a second cousin of mother's and Aunt Mary's, and asked why she didn't answer her phone.

"I didn't think it would be anyone I knew," she said, and Farley took her picture.

Her face hung like Gus's old sweat shirt on the back of the chair in his room in Kansas City.

We stayed for half an hour and left.

The Lions' Den

Gus tried to eat my dolls. I'd find an arm on the lawn, or a leg. Sometimes a rubberband and the little hooks that held the limbs together. Nealy and I chased him through the yard. Then mother'd yell at us through the window.

The Drowning at Flat Creek

July was a rainy month in Missouri. When we returned from the Carolinas, we sent to the Cornwallis on the Fourth under our umbrellas. Water was still standing on the edge of fields, and the current on the river was swift. One fisherman that Farley knew almost had drowned—caught with his line in the underbrush on a creek that was usually not over a few feet deep.

I paddled with Horace Krudup on the short float trip we took that day on Flat Creek. C.C. and Jason, who married earlier in the summer, were in another boat, and the Girards, their friends, followed them. There had been another storm in the night and water was high. It was the first day that canoes were allowed on the swollen tributary in a week.

"Horace!" I yelled. We hardly started when he let us run into the brush and low trees that hung over the creek bank. I could only lean low in the front of the canoe and try to keep from being swept out by the tug of branches over me.

"Horace!" I yelled again. I heard Jason laugh. Horace tried with a lunge to push us back into the mainstream, but he turned us over instead. The current was swift and the water cold. The canoe passed by me, and I went under a moment. The oar thumped my head—I struggled in the water—the same creek where I had been baptized by Pastor Hill. I couldn't find anything to hold on to, and went under again. The water swirled around me, and I wondered if I were passing into the death Pastor Hill spoke about. I felt the cold, wet darkness. I thought of the man who nearly drowned. Had he gone down into death and up into the resurrection? I found some branches understream and kicked against them. I came up to the air, able then to grab onto a low branch above me. I quivered with terror. The water tried to pull me under again, but I held to the branch.

"Hadley—" Horace called. "Swim to the other side of the creek. Jason has the boat." They waited on a rocky shore that jutted into the shallow side of the river. Flat Creek was not wide, nor unusually deep, but in the current, it was difficult to get across. I swam holding onto a branch that floated in the river. Horace soon joined me, and we both paddled toward our boat. We were far downstream when we got to the other side.

We walked back up the creek to them, trembling from head to foot. "Horace, if you do that once more—" my voice caught in my throat—and soaking wet, still shaking, I cried. I felt as though the man's hands that nearly drowned had been upon me.

C.C. laughed.

"I was scared, C.C.," I said. "It wasn't funny."

"It wasn't that bad, Hadley." Jason said. "We could see you all the time." But I was still mad at Horace because he had wiped out on the first curve and left me hanging in the brush.

"I lost my oar, Horace," I said. "You'll have to guide the boat by yourself."

"Maybe one of the other boats will pick it up," he said.

My body was weak as we turned the canoe over and emptied it of its load of water. I had a rip in my shirt and scratches on my arms and legs.

Horace and I got back into the canoe and started down Flat Creek again. "Tie your bag to the seat of the canoe," I called to C.C., "in case you turn over." I pushed the wet hair from my forehead with a trembling hand.

"Anyone stupid enough to bring their purse on a float trip deserves to lose it." Jason said and C.C. glared at him.

Horace guided our canoe through another

curve and the first rapids. I held on tightly because we nearly went over again. My fingers ached, I held so hard to the sides of the canoe.

Horace laughed. "Hadley's stiff as a broom holding onto the boat—" He yelled to Jason to look at me.

"Better than letting you drown me," I said. I was through with Horace. I saw the Girards far ahead, but the river curved again and I lost sight of them.

There were other people on the river that day. The sun warmed my back and I was beginning to dry as we went through another small rapids. It was still twelve miles to Peavine Landing.

I thought again of the water that flowed over me when I was in Flat Creek, and I remembered Farley's pictures he had taken July Fourth for the *Chronicle*—the shallow flow of water over Hammergies fields—puddles on the road. He took rain dripping from a barn roof and birds on a telephone wire. The Cornwallis had two pages in the *Chronicle*. I would miss all of that if I drowned.

I thought of Aunt Mary as we rowed the current that day. "Wasn't I trying to row upstream when the current pulled down?" She asked when I had not wanted to go to church with her. There had been loud arguments between us. But I couldn't go Aunt Mary's downstream ways. Church was her byword, her *shibboleth*. Anyone who was not on the second row in Hammergies Church was a fugitive from God and should be corrected. But her downstream was upstream for me. I had to go against the current within me, not with it, to sit in the church.

We came beside C.C. and Jason in their canoe. C.C. must have thought we were going to ram them. She quit paddling, leaned back, and their canoe turned over when it went sideways in the current. They were in shallow water, and soon they were on the shore emptying their canoe. We rowed on, and when they caught up with us, they were arguing again.

Usually, I could walk across Flat Creek, but rain had made it deep. "We have drought, or we drown," Aunt Mary had exclaimed as she made grape preserves in her kitchen.

I sat in the back of the canoe as Horace guided from the front. The float trips had once been fun for us—turning over one another in the creek—the churt and chortle of the birds from the slow passing trees along the bank. But now I wanted to reach Peavine Landing when it would be over.

We were on the deep side of the creek or in the shallows. Sometimes we turned sideways and then we were backwards. I was irritated with the way Horace rowed the canoe. He was tired also of the trip. And I could hear C.C. and Jason behind us. The current seemed swifter around the next bend and I heard another rapids ahead. We saw a canoe turn over. Two men were trying to get it to shore.

"C.C. and I could row together if I had an oar," I said to Horace, "and you and Jason——"

"Let them fight," he said. "They asked for it."

"How do you mean?"

"They got married, didn't they?"

C.C. and Jason's friends, the Girards, were waiting ahead. We came upon them quickly. "Your oar?" He called from the shallows where they had stopped.

"Yes, thank goodness," I said. Now I would have it for the rapids ahead. Horace rowed the canoe toward them, but missed, and they had to come after us holding the oar out until I got ahold of it.

"When it floated past, Janice thought it might be yours." Girard tried to stop C.C. and Jason, but they rowed past us on the deeper side of Flat Creek. "Slow down," he yelled. "A man on the bank said there's been an accident downstream."

Jason waved as they started down the rapids. Horace said that he didn't know if Jason had heard Girard in the roar of rushing water.

I thought a man must have drowned, a fisherman or someone turned over in a canoe and caught underneath. It happened once, sometimes several times a year. I felt my fear again. That was it, after all. I remembered what Farley told me about Bill.

In the second World War, Farley had been in the supply depot while Bill was in the field. "Bill found a malevolence he never forgot that keeps him hamstrung to Ann and the God-preaching Mary Corder," Farley said.

Horace and I tried to steer the canoe through the rapids. Behind us, the Girards had turned over, but I saw they were upright again.

Ahead of us there was a crowd on the shore. Jason had stopped and I saw Thomas Grostephan and others I knew. Then I saw the body on the ground—rescuers around it were still in a daze. Someone got up and tried to revive the body again, but it looked useless.

Horace pulled the boat into the shore. "I don't want to see it, Horace." I said.

"It's a woman, Hadley," he answered. "Stay in the boat."

"You gave up too soon," the man said who still knelt over the woman.

"You bring her back then."

"It's too late. You should have kept trying. We've waited too long."

The men still breathed quickly. One of them still worked over the body.

"It won't do any good."

"—the rescue unit." I heard someone say.

"She's dead."

"It's been called—it'll take a while to get here though."

I saw the limp body—feet pointing out, legs bent in haphazard manner—"When life is gone, the body's like a rubber tire on the shore." It didn't matter what the legs did. I tried not to look, but my head kept turning back to it, staring at the woman.

She looked captured in some strange way. I quivered and turned away again, feeling a sick headache coming, and wished I wasn't with Horace Krudup that day.

I heard the men argue again over what to do. They bent over the drowned woman again. It was awkward to know there was nothing they could do. They touched her, and I heard the lungs gurgle. How could it be a woman?

"Are you all right?" Thomas Grostephan asked.

"Yes," I said. "—No, I'm not." I changed my mind. "I've never seen a drowned body." I told him. "It looks so bloated and gray. There're noises—" I turned away. "And those little bite marks—"

"Who is she?"

"I don't know."

"Was she with anyone?"

Thomas sat down by the boat. "I don't know, Hadley."

I swallowed and tried to talk again. "I would like to be someplace far away—" I said, "as far away as the Adriatic Sea."

Thomas sat with me a while on the boat. Soon we heard the siren of the rescue unit coming up the highway from Hammergies. Then I saw Jason's boat pulled on the shore. Once in a while I could hear C.C. scream.

The Porch Swing

The alfalfa sun wheezed through the yard trees, and the slats of the porch swing marked the back of mother's legs when she went into the house for lemonade. Gus would push us then, until the swing bumped against the porch rail with a thud-thud that jarred the house, and Aunt Mary would call from the kitchen where mother squeezed the summer into narrow glasses with the rasp and screak of the swing. She wore shorts then, but not since, and the momentary markings on her legs slatted the years as I waited on the porch swing for the bump of sun through the trees.

Jam Up Creek

Telephone wires along the road to Columbia. Trucks and buses on the high and narrow bridge across the Missouri River to Booneville. Bill wouldn't stop because he didn't want to lose our place in line.

The Abstraction of War

They turned around and drove off—Bill, Nealy and mother. I watched them from the window of my room when they went back to Kansas City after we unloaded the car, and they left me at the University of Missouri with my belongings in a small room. I saw people in the street under my window that I didn't know, but they seemed to know one another. They talked in groups and stopped to talk. I didn't know anyone but Jane Newpher, and I called her. We walked downtown together. I don't know why I hadn't thought to room with someone I knew from high school.

We had waited for Farley before we left Kansas City but he didn't come. I knew he was out taking pictures.

"Sidetracked—" Gus had said.

"No, Gus. He was on track." I answered. "We are the sidetrack for him." Farley and his cameras were his interest. Family didn't mean much to him. But I thought he should have come that day I left for school.

I had a headache when Jane and I got back to the dormitory, and I went to sleep, until my roommate, who had just come in, woke me and startled, I looked at her with a pounding head.

That fall at the university, I went to classes under the large, yellow trees on campus without Nealy, Gus, Farley, father, Mary Corder or mother. The streets were crowded with students, yet I still knew none of them. Nealy had always been my best friend, but she had another year in high school. She wasn't coming to the university anyway.

I sat in the lecture halls and took notes. It was like being broken, taken to the bone. It was like the steep drive at the back of our house down into the basement where Bill parked the car. Mother wouldn't drive it into the basement because the incline was too steep. As children, we would scream when the car went down the drive. I felt slid into a place like the car under our old house in Kansas City, the house we had always had. Even when we moved to Indiana for a short time, Farley had lived in it for us.

The yellow fall spread itself like honey on the campus. I remembered our house where we sat on the front porch in the evenings. Also Aunt Mary's house where mother made her pale lemonade. Angels stalked the attic when it got dark, and left us mauled under the stairs by morning.

I wanted to study journalism at the university but I could only take required freshman courses, and I didn't want to study them. "You've got to be informed if you want to write—" Bill called when my grades got bad. I rode behind a boy on a motorcycle on a highway south of Columbia. We sat on a bluff at the Missouri River and talked. I brought my books, but didn't study.

I wanted to live on the river bluff. The sun like a flash of Farley's camera blinked on the water. Its light, as if a nimbus behind some Christ's head, also spilled from the clouds. Gus's old dreams of birds flew from the attic.

The yellow trees shed their leaves around us on the university campus. "I failed another test." I told Jane Newpher as we walked to the dormitory that day. "It was harder than I thought it would be. I know I failed."

When I was in my room thinking about my grades, I heard my buzzer, which meant I had a visitor. "Farley's here." I told my roommate. "I know it's him."

I went downstairs to the main floor of the dormitory and Farley stood at the desk with a camera over his shoulder.

"Somehow I knew it was you, maybe only hoped it was. But your name was the first that came to my head when I heard my buzzer."

"I need some pictures for the *Chronicle*." He said. "Have you gotten around yet?"

"Yes—to a cave in Easley which you would like. It's one store beside the railroad track."

"Let's go."

"It's on the river too. But Farley, I have studying to do—American Government and I'm not doing well in that class."

"There's nothing hard about a course in government," he said. "We'll study on the way. I won't be here long. I'm on my way to Whalen River to fish."

We drove south from Columbia to a turn-off which I told him to follow. We climbed the river bluff and Farley took my picture as I sat at the mouth of the cave and looked at my government book. He took the light from inside the cave. He took the shimmering river, the sunlight through the last of the yellow leaves. He took the patterns of dried mud and dust on his jeep.

"Now Nealy is alone with her," we talked of mother, "but she could always do better with her than me. Farley," I paused as I showed him the turn when we left the store that was Easley, Missouri. "I think my grades are going to be bad. I'm behind in studying and the classes just keep moving ahead and I don't have time to catch up. Mother wouldn't like the things I do. Aunt Mary would go into orbit."

Farley laughed as we drove back to Columbia to find a place to eat.

"I like it at the university, Farley. If only I can stay in school until I get to journalism."

Comeuppance

I went off to the University of Missouri like a stretched rubber band that Gus let fly from his thumb and fingers. Now after the first semester, I had to go back and struggle with my failures. "I would be the rest of my years in college bringing up that low grade-average," mother said, but I wanted to study journalism.

"Gus quit the University of Kansas City." Bill held up his index finger. "Hadley is on probation at the University of Missouri." He raised his second finger. "Nealy is going to Bible College and wants to be a missionary." He held up his third finger and we looked at one another in the small living room with a border around the wall that mother wanted him to change. Bill was a pragmatic newsman covering labor disputes and we were giving ourselves away for nothing.

Bill put his head in his hands and cried before us in his chair. We hadn't seen him cry before. I was afraid he'd start yelling at us the way he did mother. Gus would fly and Nealy would suck my hair. I was getting ready to leave again for school and wanted to finish packing my suitcase, but we stayed in our chairs.

The Iron Boot

Going back to the University of Missouri in the fall for the second year was nearly like drowning in Flat Creek. But I wanted to work at the *Chronicle* and Mr. Creveling, the editor, said I would need a journalism degree if I wrote for him. It was hard to be without Nealy again, back in school, knowing that Bill Williges and Mr. Creveling of the *Chronicle* probably had exerted pressure on the school to take me back.

I had to make myself study, but my head was full of mother. The university called for a smooth road, but I knew potholes and detours. I waited as long as I could to go to classes. I put off coming back to the dormitory after classes to read the assignments and study.

Once I hitch-hiked outside Columbia and let a stranger have me.

Bill called me several times the first months to ask how I was doing.

"It's not hard yet," I said, "since I'm taking two classes over again."

I would have to go to summer school, "if I made it that far," mother said.

I visited the journalism school in Neff and Williams Hall in the Quadrangle after class on Fridays to talk. Then Thomas Grostephan, from Hammergies, took me to dinner one Saturday night. I asked if Aunt Mary had called Winifred, his mother, and told her to tell him to take me out. I had the thought that anyone who did anything for me, did it because they knew I hadn't made it my first year and my parents, or Aunt Mary, had asked them.

"One day of study would be added to another," Aunt Mary wrote, "like members of the early church. That church formed after Christ departed from the earth, went forward one step at a time, with nothing they went, without so much as a map and sometimes against their will, they were driven from place to place because of their faith, not always moving by choice but chased from Jerusalem, they preached Jesus through the resurrection of the dead and were put in custody until the next day, and many of them who heard the word believed and then they, too, were scattered from Judea, to Samaria, as far as Phoenicia and Antioch"—chased from their flat-roofed houses where stalks of flax were left when they were chased along the roads, nubby as feedsacks in the grain store in Hammergies—yes, because of faith, they were driven careless as the boy that drove the motorcycle when I felt the wind in my face. He didn't have another helmet that Friday I broke loose from school for a late afternoon at the Missouri River bluffs. I closed my eyes and put my head against his back without a book to study. I only wanted to run like the early Christians, but I ran on purpose, unlike them, who fled because they tried to establish Christianity in every place they could—Hammergies and Kansas City and Columbia, where I hadn't looked, but ran, with Jonah, the forerunner of all—and the early Christians on their motorcycles headed for the Missouri autumn and the river bluffs I liked to climb. I knew the windbreaks burned and wind would have the soil. We stopped at Easley's store where I saw a fish just caught as it gulped for air on the bench in front. I saw its silvery scales, its fins and flopping tail, its round, black eye—and its mouth gulping for air like it was saying, "Hope. Hope. Hope."

Fuller Man

"In the book of Isaiah, after the reign of Solomon, the Hebrew people were divided into two nations: Israel and Judah, and there was a civil war between them. Ahaz was king of Judah and Pekah was king of Israel.

"Now Pekah joined Rezin, king of Syria. Ahaz was afraid of the two kings. But the prophet, Isaiah, met him at the conduit of the upper pool in the highway of the fuller's field and told Ahaz not to worry. Isaiah prophesied they would not defeat him."

Pastor Hill looked at me as he preached that Sunday night in the Hammergies Church. I had come to Aunt Mary's the weekend before finals to study and hear her pray. Even Nealy and mother had come. But a headache raged in my head all day. I still had to return to Columbia that night. Thomas Grotesphan would give me a ride.

"The Christian stands on the highway in the fuller's field." Pastor Hill was somewhere in his sermon when I listened again. "We belong to the Fuller Man, the Cleaner Man. The Lord himself." I tried to follow Pastor Hill. "Who shall stand when He appears?" Pastor Hill's voice filled the church. "The Lord is a refiner's fire and a fuller's soap."

"Amen," Aunt Mary stood and raised her hands.

"Hallo-loo-yuh." Pastor Hill called me to the altar. Aunt Mary and the elders put their hands on me. "Unwind the dark road before her," Pastor Hill boomed. "Loose the headache." I felt his hands quake my head, split my skull. I felt the pavement of my brain unfork. The long, curved road stretched to heaven like a tongue. I could see the way back to Columbia later that night. Buckets of Jesus's blood washed over me like rain. My brain uncoiled in long rows of intestines. My old headaches bucked. Every one I'd ever had. I felt Jesus, the Fuller Man, stomp his foot on the headaches that ran like lice from my open head. Holy. Holy. They prayed in the answers I needed for exams.

Ax Murder

Bill was gone with Farley for the newspaper and in the spring rain, weeds had grown up around the mock-orange bush and around the other bushes between ours and the neighbors' yards. Nealy and I pulled weeds by Farley's overturned dinghy and in the four o'clocks by the backstairs. Mother thought Bill would trim the shrubs and clear the overgrown brush in the backyard with her when he got back to Kansas City for the weekend, but on Saturday, Farley came in his field pants and camouflage jacket.

"What are you doing?" Mother asked.

Bill stood with Farley in the backyard. He pushed his finger along his nose. "—thought I'd go fishing."

"You've been gone with him all week," Mother snorted. "You've got things to do."

Farley looked at the yard.

"I'll do them later." Bill said.

Mother stood in his way.

"Ann, you're pushing—"

"It's you who's pushing." She said. "I do everything around here. You come and go whenever you want."

"I'm going now." He pushed by her.

I looked at Nealy.

When Bill left with Farley, mother went into the house, and returned to the yard with an ax in her hand. I reached for Nealy as mother lifted the ax. She came down on Farley's dinghy, chopping at it again and again until she made a hole. She kept chopping until she splintered the boards. She chopped until she splattered the dinghy over the yard.

"What'd you do that for?" Gus came to the backyard.

"Shudup," she said in her fury, and stomped into the house.

"Well—we've got firewood for winter," Nealy said and we laughed.

Nealy

I sat on the treestump sawed off from Nealy in the heat of missionary journeys. Nealy stirred in church, her spirit, wind. I was the log, the stump. I would think of her burning by the fireplace like coals when she got to jumping on the hallelujah wave that took her dark to Africa.

The Obituaries

After her two years of Bible College, Nealy wrote to us from the missionary-compound in Africa. Mother cried when her letters came. I did also. I sat at the *Chronicle* under the shade tree of Bill and Farley Williges, while Nealy burned in the sun and wind of Nigeria.

I dated Thomas Grostephan and worked in obituaries with Margaret Crussel at the *Chronicle* when I graduated from the University of Missouri.

"Yes," she said, "go on—" A grieving widow had called about her husband's death. "Well, there's another one gone," Crussel hung up the phone, and typed the death-notice for the paper.

"When did he die?" Another call had come. "How do you spell the name?" There was a pause, and I supposed the widow was crying. "I've got work to do," Crussel said, "you'll have to get on with it."

Crussel was indifferent to sorrow and grief— the death of a mother's child—a spinster's last relative with whom she'd lived for years—Crussel had heard it all.

*   *   *

After a few months in the desert of Crussel's obituaries, Farley took me with him.

Hadley Williges

"You had the fortitude to finish college," Farley said. We were covering politics in southern Missouri in February when we upturned a meeting of the Ku Klux Klan. I was discouraged over work at the *Chronicle*. They thought I was hired because I was a Williges instead of a reporter. "Work then," dad told me, "so they'll know the difference." But I had nearly died in the obituaries with Crussel and I couldn't decide if traveling with Farley were a step forward or back.

I waited in the back of the building while Farley inched his way behind a stage and took the men at the meeting. I waited to hear him knock something over, but he finished his work.

"We circle the sun, Farley, and not the sun, us." I said when we were back in the car.

"What does that mean?" Farley puffed on his pipe.

"Because you reject that way and build other ways, you think that alters the way?"

"Nealy been writing you again, Mary Corder?" He asked. "I remember when you didn't feel that way."

"I found I was only able to fail on my own. I can't write like Bill. The *Chronicle* doesn't need anyone else but you taking pictures. Africa doesn't need me."

He watched the country as we talked. His favorite camera, which he called "the Stieglitz," was beside him.

"I can't get a story," I said with the pencil and paper still on my lap.

"It takes time. Bill and I have been at it for twenty-five years."

"Politics doesn't interest me."

"It doesn't have to. Just listen to the candidates, interview people, condense what they say—give it a point. You just don't have the discipline yet for writing."

"While you can't have discipline, Farley," I said. "For your work, you have to be loose—You have to be free to make your leaps of imagination—and I'm not you either, Farley. And don't tell me about discipline. When have you ever done any-thing you didn't want to?"

Farley laughed.

"Writing for the *Chronicle* is dealing with the ordinary—giving order to something that doesn't deserve the effort. Now, Farley, it's not that you and Bill don't turn up the salamander on Elephant Rock, because you do—and often with you, there's more than the ordinary, but what does politics in southern Missouri have to do with Kansas City to the north-east?"

Farley developed his pictures at the newspaper office in Pilot Knob where we'd come that evening while I wrote some shallow words for the *Chronicle*.

Farley handed me a picture while I was still writing the story. When she wasn't aware that Farley was watching, he took a picture of the wife of one of the candidates as she looked down from the platform where she stood with her husband. The look on her face could be seen all the way through the camera into a page of the paper, where she could look down on everyone.

"You got her, Farley," I said.

"Cornstarch," he said.

I shook my head.

"Humanity is what you're after in southern Missouri, Hadley."

We moved on in the morning. We'd been in St. Francois County, would travel to Iron and New Madrid counties.

"Do you ever get sued, Farley?"

"For taking the truth?"

"For uncovering what should be left covered."

"You think there's a law?"

"I'll ask Thomas Grostephan when we get back to Kansas City."

"What would he know about it?"

"He's a lawyer."

"He just finished law school. He's nothing more than a clerk in that law office."

In Gads Hill, where we'd come for the night, I thought of Nealy. The sky had been heavy and gray before dark. "We ought to listen to the news, Farley," I said, "and leave town."

But Farley never heard the radio and television. Newspapers were the only form of communication for him. It snowed that night and the next day.

"Farley, pick up your socks." We were still in our rooms in Gads Hill Hotel. When I knocked for

Farley in the morning, pushed open his door, I thought the storm had come up in the night in his room.

"And you ought to lock your door, Farley," I told him. "Someone might write a story on how you live."

We drove into the snow falling around us.

"Moholy-Nagy," Farley said.

"I think of the upstairs of our house with Gus and Nealy. We'd lift the window in the snow and call the angels."

"Object and space battle for the camera." Farley hardly made sense as his concentration got ahold of him. He talked about the relationship of object and space to the ground and the frame of his Stieglitz.

Farley took pictures of a white church speckled with snow—the same sky and winter printed fields. While we were at the church, a man drove up. "The church organist," he said, "come to see that the church was closed." They had people break in sometimes at night, he said as Farley took his picture.

We went in the church with him, and looked around the room, but Farley still took pictures of the man.

"I thought object and space battled for the camera," I said.

"Humanity comes first, Hadley," Farley reminded me. "The history of photography begins with people and ends that way."

The books of Civil War photographs and old portraits on the bookshelf in Farley's apartment crossed my mind.

"Peacher," the man said his name was, as Farley took another picture of him at the window of the church. The snow sifted by his head and the light fell across his bleak face and caught his lip as he said, "Peacher."

Then we went back outside while Farley took more pictures. "The white peak of the church will be in the *Chronicle* beside the white peak of the Ku Klux Klan hat."

"You can't, Farley."

"I can," he said. "They'll be with other photos of the rural southern Missouri snowstorm."

I looked at Farley with indignation and wondered if his finger still clicked while he slept.

The snow turned hard in the cold and gray-brown on the roads. It was a harsh cold as we came down the steep hill back to town. We would have moved on, but the highways were closed and it took two men by the curb to get Farley's jeep into the ice ruts where he parked it for the night. Then we went, frozen, into the hotel as the red sun on the horizon, like hope that we would leave Gads Hill, went down into the dark.

The Mexican Stand-off

It was strange that Farley should talk about humanity and have a collection of war photographs, I thought at breakfast in the Gads Hill Hotel. He stayed away from relationships with people and his war experience was in the supply-depot. Were those his interests because he was only an observer? He had to have his camera between him and the world?

"Well, Farley," I said, "humanity for you is what can be seen by the eye—filtered through your way of seeing—your style. But humanity for me, is what cannot be seen. It's the faith of the church organist. It's Mary Corder's stand for the Lord. It's even mother's passion for the family, when it hasn't brought her much pleasure."

Farley threw his hands in the air.

"And humanity is Nealy, who like Moses, drank at the sun."

"Does saying the words, 'I accept Jesus Christ as my Savior,' change me?"

"Yes, Farley, it does."

"I wish you and Mary Corder would find something else to harp on—" Farley said, lifting the blue coffee cup, spilling a little over the rim as he drank.

"The stone the builders rejected, is become the cornerstone."

Farley, like Juan Piccola at the *Chronicle*, resolved that statement the only way he could, by rejecting the God who said it.

After breakfast, Farley took pictures of men in the barbershop of the hotel talking politics, while I stood at the door and smelled their cheroot and the eucalyptus of Farley's pipe. There was a fern in the hall of the old hotel.

"Photography was an object seen through the rectangle of a frame in a given point of time," Farley had said, "not abstractions and unrecognizable forms as some photographers had done."

I waited for Farley awhile, then returned to my room to work on the story of politics.

*   *   *

The snow was cold and confining. Ice under the snow was hard. I saw Farley from the window of the hotel with his cameras, his head thrown back in the weather. It had been a heavy snow. It was as though the cold had a hold on the town and would not let go, while the captivity we suffered and the humanity Farley chased, separated in inverse proportion. I returned to my bed where I read the Gideon Bible and waited for Farley to remember that he had me with him.

Piecemeal

Wednesday we were able to travel to New Madrid. "We should go back to Kansas City," I told Farley, "I don't want to be stuck in another town." We were almost the only traffic on the road.

But Farley had not finished taking his pictures and I did not have my story. We came to New Madrid at night, "tired like the apostle Paul must have been when he came to Ephesus with Priscilla and Aquila," I mumbled.

"Where did you find them?" Farley asked.

"I read about them in the Gideon Bible in Gads Hill."

But Paul, like Farley, could only stay in one place a short while, and left his fellow tent-makers to go on to other places—as Farley would do.

When Farley developed his pictures that night, I saw another turn to his artistry. The humanity he took began to relate to shapes and other objects in his pictures. The men in the barber chairs in Gads Hill leaned to one another as they talked, in the same angle as the ferns he took in the hall of the hotel.

And while Priscilla and Aquila made tents in Ephesus, they heard a man preach—but it was John the Baptist that they preached, and much had happened since John—Jesus having come and gone—while the man must have been in the backhills, they supposed. They called him over to them and expounded God to him through Jesus Christ our Lord.

I couldn't find Farley when the *Chronicle* called. "Who knows where he is?" I asked the editor, who was angry with us anyway because it had taken him a while to track us down.

And talking to Mr. Creveling, I gave him what I had on politics in southern Missouri, but I knew, like the man who preached John the Baptist, I didn't have it all.

The Photographer

The sun was up in the morning as we left New Madrid. I rode in Farley's jeep as it jumped the ice ruts on the old road we took from town. He stopped at the hoary roots of an arthritic tree that held to an embankment along the road. He took pictures of the knotted roots; and squares of the fence-wire were like the iron ghost of an old quilt.

Farley took humps of dirt along the fence, pencil rows of stubbled fields where snow wore thin.

By mid-day, the thaw was running patterns of wet and dry cement across the road we traveled, like little ghosts wandering from children in the old schoolyard.

At the end of the field by Holopeter, Missouri, a stumpy tree stood with two posts like Father, Son and Holy Ghost.

Tall clumps of weeds, several broken, bent across the others—

red clay creekbank,

redbrown edge of snow,

trees cut through

for utility wires stretched from pole to pole—

at last, we were on our way back to Kansas City.

The Quartet at Trinity Church

Farley took pictures of the quartet concert for the *Chronicle:* lute, harpsicord, recorder, guitar.

Matthew, Mark, Luke, and John, were there, straight as pipes of the organ on the wall—and others, David or Paul—but stained glass hid its scenes at night. I also thought of Aunt Mary. "Trinity is shaped like a cross," I said during the concert, "like the church in Hammergies."

The crowd of people in the church pressed upon Farley. "Tell me, Hadley, what do you see?"

"My headaches in the crown of thorns—the camera that carries your seed and brings forth your sons."

We stood quietly behind the stone pier under the iron work of a side-aisle lamp. Farley shot the stone floor, wood pew, cross and pier.

It was as though Jesus stepping from Galilee for a moment when I heard the lute and harpsichord.

I saw the organ pipes from the balcony stand forward like a ship's rigging. The church held the chambered music as we listened. "How can we not sail, Farley, in the heavy church and with the diversity of the multitudes. Even the Bible is a collection of versions. Look at the four gospels. Do they agree?"

Farley's camera clicked the quartet and took a child by his grandmother, his coat on backward, the hood up over his face.

"You could light the sea's dark weight for us."

"I could never walk on water, Hadley," he said.

When She Stopped Screaming

The neighbors said if they heard the voices of my parents one more time they'd turn up their radios loud as they could. They'd ring our phone at night. They'd call the police. They'd sign petitions call the moving van. They'd organize vigilantes to get us out of town—

How could she leave a house she'd lived in all

her married life? Mother screamed back. Her children raised there.

Upstairs, Gus rattled his marble collection in Farley's tobacco tins until mother rushed into his room.

When she left, he crawled under his bed, buried them in the insulation under his attic floor.

The Coliseum of The Cornfield

"I don't want to go to the far edge where Bill and Farley have gone for their work," I told Thomas Grostephan after work. "I've had enough," I said with a headache.

We sat in The Cornfield, a dark tavern tucked into a corner of a building on a backstreet near the *Chronicle*. I talked to Thomas and watched Farley and Bill farther away from us at the bar, surrounded by newspaper people talking loudly.

Farley in a fit, jumped over the bar for another bottle of beer. The newspaper people who saw him cheered, and he looked at me. "It's disgusting," I said to Thomas and looked away, holding my fingers to my headache while Farley trumpeted by caws of the black bird night, jumped fenceposts, hurdled tree-stumps in The Cornfield.

"Let's go then," Thomas said.

Their voices were like the thick in the neck of old milk bottles, holding back the milk a moment before it surged into the cereal bowl and over the edge like cries from a circus or a battlefield.

I could hear mother yell as Thomas held me—Bill pecking at the typewriter downstairs in his room like it was full of inmates beating their tin cups against the bars of their cells.

Politics

"What do you want to get married for?" Farley asked. It was to be the first wedding since Ann and Bill. "I usually don't do weddings," he said.

"Neither do I."

"It's never been anything but a grinding stone." I said to Farley.

"And you're asking for more of the same?" Farley shrugged. "Stay loose. I've been once too often to flute school."

"I've seen enough photographers leaping over

bars to know what it is to be loose." He irritated me. "You've never been able to stand still. —Freedom, Farley," I told him, "is the ability to do what you know you have to."

Thomas Grostephan

Farley was late to the wedding. He rushed into the door of the church with a kerchief tied around his head. He'd been drinking the night before, and was still in bed in Kansas City when Bill called him an hour before the ceremony.

"Well, you made it again," I said flatly.

He looked at me. "Don't give me grief, Hadley."

I could tell by his face that he was sick. He usually didn't drink as much as he must have the night before. His style was off as he knelt before Bill and me in the aisle and took pictures of the wedding ceremony.

The smell of white gladiolus surrounded me in the Hammergies Church, with the presence of the wedding guests and Farley's trembling camera.

He stood at the end of the long aisle as I walked

toward the foot of the cross in the church with Thomas Grostephan after the wedding and smiled at me only faintly.

Mother frowned at the tribal mask Nealy sent from Africa. How could Nealy stand such a place, she asked, different from everything we knew?

"Hadley, I'm happy to see you marry Thomas," Aunt Mary said at the reception. She stood by mother with her arm around him. Thomas kissed her cheek. I turned to open another wedding present.

Jason and C.C. stopped to talk to me. "We're going to have another reception in Kansas City for the newspaper people and Thomas's law friends. Then I'm sure mother will want one at our church there." Hertess and Winifred Grostephan, Thomas's aunt and mother, pressed between us with more Hammergies friends and distant relatives.

I turned to greet them with the kiss of Farley's camera lens.

The Pictures

"The *Wall Street Journal*?" I walked into Farley's cubicle after I returned to work at the *Chronicle*. He had been distant as Gus since the wedding last month.

"There's an article on Andre Kertesz?"

"A photographer?" I asked after a silence.

"One of the best. He has an exhibit at a gallery in New York." Farley said. "I'm going to order the book of his pictures."

I looked over Farley's shoulder and read. "Native Hungary. Two roosters lower their heads to battle. A couple with back to the camera peek through a crack in a fence at a circus. The plain geometry of the fence—"

"Do you have the wedding pictures?"

"What?" He asked.

"The wedding pictures. It's been nearly a month."

"They're in the file cabinet," he nodded absent-mindedly.

I looked through the drawer, unable to find them.

Farley was absorbed by the article.

"Mother's angry you're taking so long."

He continued to read.

"Farley, the pictures—" I insisted.

"They're in the file cabinet." He didn't look up.

"Where in the cabinet? I don't understand your filing system."

He got up from the chair, came to the cabinet and jerked open the bottom drawer. "In that manila envelope, Mrs. Grostephan." He returned to his chair.

"They're lovely, Farley," I said.

"Just took pictures like I was instructed to do."

"My mouth is open too far in that one." I looked through the pictures. "I was smiling at Thomas—"

"Kertesz photographed a man in a bathing suit whose image was distorted by natural light refracting through water." Farley ignored me.

"That appeals to an old bread-and-butter photographer like you?"

"Yes," he admitted. "And he experimented with female nudes—he distorted—made surreal— with erotic charges." Farley looked at me.

"Why don't you go to New York to see the

exhibit? I've never been to New York. Why don't we both go?"

"You're married, Hadley. What would your husband say?" Farley slammed the book and lit his pipe. "Your mouth is open too far." He watched me going through the wedding pictures. "You like them?"

"Yes, Farley, I do. But there're more of me than anyone else."

"You were the bride."

"Yes, but Thomas was the groom. Wasn't he there too?" I asked. "You experimented with the gladiolus." I looked at Farley's pictures of crisscrossing leaves, sword-like, and the spikes of flowers.

He put his pipe in his mouth. "I take what's there to take."

I kept looking through the photographs.

"Gus called." Farley told me.

"What about? He never calls us."

"He wanted me to take pictures of the rally they're having."

"What'd you say?"

"I told him I didn't do political cartoons."

In the Pecan Grove

"How do you like being married?" Farley asked as we rode in his jeep.

"Nealy's gone. We don't have Gus to dinner because he doesn't like Thomas. You and Thomas don't speak. The few friends I remember from school are scattered or I have nothing in common with them now."

"You're the one with the freedom to do what has to be done."

I didn't say anything for awhile.

"Let's stop here in the pecan grove. I know you like pecans."

"It's starting to rain, Farley."

"Look at that woman gathering nuts in the rain," he said, and got his cameras.

The sky was clear, yet behind the sun, a slight rain came from a small cloud. An old woman with a long skirt over her knees and a crooked hand holding a pail gathered pecans in the grove. Farley went to take her picture while I waited in the jeep. She looked up just at that moment with a girlish grin about to come out on her face.

For a moment she forgot she was old and a man

was coming toward her. I watched Farley coax the grin from her.

"I didn't know you was looking at me." I heard her say.

"Yes you did," Farley said, and she laughed.

How did he see what the rest of us didn't notice? Farley brought out the girl in her. The girl she hadn't been for sixty years.

Lunch

Farley took me to lunch one day at The Cornfield a month before I was to have a baby.

"I didn't think I'd see you like this."

"Don't Farley. It's hard enough without your comments," I said in the noisy tavern.

"We make our own bed." He sipped his beer.

I stood.

"All right," he said.

"Hadley!" Hertha called.

I waved at her.

"How do you feel?" Dad sat with us awhile.

"How's the story?" I asked instead. I ate the

pastrami sandwich when Getta brought it to the table.

"Beer, Hadley?" Farley asked.

"Milk."

The Chance

"I was supposed to follow God," mother and Aunt Mary said, "ignore my own will," which pulled at me like Thom's cry in the other room. I was a wife, and now a mother. I wanted to go my own way, like Farley. "But I had other responsibilities," they said.

I couldn't see God, yet I believed there was such a thing as salvation through faith in Jesus Christ, "and being saved," Aunt Mary reminded me, "I had made that commitment." And yet—

Thomas had already left for his law office. I let Thom cry. From the bedroom window, the morning sky had a red tinge like the side of a trout.

The Front Porch

It must be light from Galilee reflected in the corner of the porch. Aunt Mary's house in Hammergies faced west and at evening filled with sun which came from Tyre and Sidon and from beyond the Jordan.

Still the sun flamed through the trees while I rocked Thom on the porch swing, away from Thomas and Kansas City. I waited for another child I had not expected.

Mother was happy. "Maybe Hadley will stay away from Farley and the *Chronicle* now," she said.

Pastor Hill told me that a woman's place was to have children and make a home. I was to sit in his church and not think, but do only what my husband told me. No wonder I couldn't connect with Thomas. No wonder I wanted out. I was to teach Sunday school. Serve God. Where was the Christ who stilled the waters and walked on waves? Where was the Christ who turned the world on its nose and loosed the heavy bands?

Maybe that was it. The gospel put us in bondage, then the miracle of it was that we could survive in that bondage.

That was the hope of the gospel?

I rocked Thom on Aunt Mary's porch.

What could we talk about? Her love of Christ? The box she'd lived in all her life? What could she tell me? I wished I was with Farley roiling over backroads. Seeing my words in the morning paper. What could Aunt Mary know?

The Headache

Gus had made angels out of sticks from the woodpile. We burned them in the fireplace while Bill and mother yelled in the kitchen. Just before the fire ate the angels, their wings looked as if they moved. We knew they were flying. Sometimes before they faded, we could hear a high whine like air forced through a small opening between two panes of glass.

I felt the angels burning in my head. I had another headache coming. I held my hands that fluttered like the angels' wings.

Gravity

Aunt Mary told us Anna Ruth was in the hall—her sister who'd been dead fifty years.

I'd heard it first in church, Aunt Mary's mind would wander and she'd read the wrong words in the doxology. Then during the hymns, I'd hear her sing other words.

More often anymore, I knew she had her own course, like the sky when it falls, is drawn by the gravity of the earth.

Second Birth

"We're here to get caught," Pastor Hill paced as he preached. "We're here to get pulled out of the water. If we don't know what it is to gulp for air, we're not born again."

I felt labor pains in my stomach at the end of church. I squirmed uncomfortably. The waters swayed. The fish hook caught. Later that night, I pulled her squirming and crying, onto dry land.

Part II

Aunt Mary

The windowpane was frosted the sudden morning in December. The gray dawn tramped through the dead leaves that blew in the yard.

The frost was thick on the windowpane, in the cold morning the roads converged into the horizon.

We had tramped through the snowfields at Larned with the dead leaves. But now, my husband and two children, Thom and Jennifer, and I drove to Hammergies for Aunt Mary's death. Cars and trucks talked on Citizen's Band radios. Montana Goose and Rusty Bucket across the trails of their vernacular. Trucks and cars had lightning rods like barns.

And she would look far away, toward the Adriatic Sea, leaving her family not knowing what to do, bickering in the other room. The country in winter was dull as Aunt Mary's stories of Hammergies when they were small and hardships strung together like fields along the road. Her hair was the hedgerows when I saw her, her hands like jagged branches of the trees against the sky. She had returned to the fields when I stood above her in Hammergies.

Pastor Hill also stood at her bed.

I had brought her a book of Grandma Moses's

paintings for her rocking chair. Now she journeyed in the tracks of frost, her grave the bitter cold of the December morning. She seemed older than frost.

I heard her struggling for breath from the adjoining room where I sat on the four-poster bed and listened to mother. The sky shed a frozen mist as barter for Aunt Mary. I huffed at the window to keep the frost from leaving. Somewhere truckers talked on CB's. Rusty Bucket was nearing Iowa, on toward Council Bluffs.

I sat by Aunt Mary's bed and held her hand for awhile. She rasped like the dried grapevine on her fence in the cold wind, hands purple as when she had squeezed the grape juice through her cloth for the Lord's supper at church. She seemed to pass away as we came and went in the room, then struggled again for breath. She lasted for hours as I sat in the house and listened to the family strife that had never been resolved. They were bound together before I came into their lives.

Aunt Mary had wanted to die in her bed. But she didn't realize we would have to watch her die. She pulled at her nightgown. Her old heart ached for its rest.

I got on my knees on the plank floor and prayed

at her bed with Pastor Hill. Take Aunt Mary before she suffers. I saw her feet were veined and swollen. I covered them again with the quilt she'd pulled loose from the bed. She struggled, then was quiet again as I held her spinster hands. She didn't want to be preserved in the hospital; but even she was holding back at the end.

Aunt Mary coughed again, struggled for breath, then seemed to be unconscious again. Dad left the room unable to watch her. Mother went to call the doctor. "But what could he get?" Aunt Mary would have said before she came this far. "Another July on her church pew? Fishscales in the frost on the icepond?" She didn't want to be kept alive for nothing. She wanted to go to the Lord when it was her time.

I heard mother and dad arguing in the other room. Maybe for a united family death was bearable. I also heard Gus's sharp voice, and knew that he had come. I longed for Nealy.

I sat in the room with Aunt Mary as they hurried about, battered with words. I remember Aunt Mary's fierce scrutiny also, feeling sympathy and repugnance for her. Mother came into the room and went through Aunt Mary's closet for her Sunday dress with the collar of the embroidered grape leaves. "She would want to be buried in it," mother said.

At times, I went downstairs with the children after they came to look at her and ask if she were dead yet. Jennifer had brought me part of a snowflake she'd made at kindergarten the day before. "She had to run across the street," she explained its fragment and it had torn. She also knew frost on the window-pane and somewhere far away, truckers were on the highway. Uncle Farley took the children for a ride and said they'd have a hamburger somewhere and buy a sled at the Hammergies hardware store, if it hadn't closed. "Gunnel would open it again for them," mother said as he left with Thom and Jenni-fer hanging on his neck.

The doctor came and raised Aunt Mary on some pillows. He also gave me a prescription if I would get a headache. I'd left my medicine in Kansas City.

Aunt Mary seemed to feel better. I forgot she had to sleep raised when her heart got bad. "If she gets much worse, I'll have to take her in," he said though Aunt Mary had threatened the wrath of God upon anyone who touched her in her last hours.

But Aunt Mary, at the last, was not wanting to

go. Like mother when dad moved to Indiana when the *Chronicle* folded for a while, and she went with her arms waving backwards, as though they were wings. We had passed a moving van in the ditch somewhere along the highway in Illinois and she fluttered her arms wildly though the moving van hadn't been ours.

And I remembered the DeSoto Aunt Mary, Nealy, mother and I drove when we visited her in the summers and had traveled in Missouri—DeWitt, Rensselaer, Bevier, Polo. We had crossed the Missouri River at Waverly, up on the narrow bridge, through a cleft in the rock bluff and down Six Mile Church Road. The DeSoto knew where to go. Aunt Mary drove until they were both decrepit. I remembered the musty smell in some of the churches, the crying, wet children.

"Take the bus," Farley told her when she was getting too old to drive.

"They haven't got a bus where I want to go, Farley," she said and traveled down the roads to Perry and Buffington's grocery where she turned up her nose at the grapes, asked directions about the stone pillars of the highway—

19   E
54   E
154
YY

Thomas, my husband, came in the room. Pastor Hill came then also, as though from nowhere, and opened his Bible before the bitterness of my heart. "Lead me to the rock that is higher than me," he read from Aunt Mary's chair at the north window where I sat in the strife of family I could hear downstairs and from the adjoining room. It seemed Aunt Mary would live forever.

Thomas went downstairs and came back, saying that he and Gus were leaving for a while. He'd stay at his mother's house.

Pastor Hill took Aunt Mary's hand and prayed when she began rasping loudly again. "Give her a holy death," he said.

I looked at the windowpane with frost that would be gone like her. Fishscales in the woods of the windowpane, quail markings and woodgrain. The fir trees rejoice along the trails through snowbound fields.

Aunt Mary's eyes looked straight ahead; she

saw nothing anymore, and her breathing was fierce as it grew dark. "I'm going to take her to the hospital," the doctor said, but I felt his indecision. He called for an ambulance and Aunt Mary was taken away. She died with the coming of the morning. I doubt she knew she'd been taken from her room.

We stood with our breath steaming the bitter cold of another December morning, the wool scarf tightly around my neck. "I'm glad you have your gloves on," mother said. But I'd forgotten them.

We stood at Aunt Mary's open grave with the crowds of people from Hammergies. Jennifer held my hand. The boy was with his father. Farley was off looking at old gravestones. Mother would be angry with him later.

As we stood before Aunt Mary's grave, I heard the words Pastor Hill read for her. Cod-oil and fossils, the covering of frost our redemption in Jesus Christ so we kept going on the *amen-hallo-loo-yah-long-ride* from Hammergies. I felt the trail of highways charted by CB's and Aunt Mary far away. I was in the mud of dirtbrown hills, riding in Aunt Mary's DeSoto to Larned. "There was a way through the wilderness and a way," Nealy had said. And I covered

Aunt Mary with grape leaves, twigs, stalks of milo, sod and frost.

After the Funeral

I went to the attic where Hammergies was stored in a chatham print fourposter bed with hay-fever sickness and headache, the smell of the coal-burning stove, the cornwallis summer and Nealy with her letters from Africa.

In the attic, were frayed pages of hosannas from plowed fields. There were trunks and baskets, Aunt Mary's hat-box, books, a chest of drawers. Aunt Mary had been an elder in the Hammergies Church. Hosanna. Hosanna. The cover of her hymn book was gone. And there were droughts, a rocking chair, Isaac's well.

There were scattered remnants of the travelers that had gone on before. I found a railroad ticket in the chest of drawers and a receipt of a slave purchase at Charleston in 1852.

In the attic, the prosperous years had stored the gospel and hymn book, the altar broken down. And the armies of the living God had marched on past the house and creek, the grasses running uphill until there was only a sword, a plowshare along the road. I heard Aunt Mary's undying voice. The great army was far away.

I opened one of the journals I found in the chest of drawers and began reading. I thought it was one of the books in which she copied prayers, but it read more like a diary. "I am filled with doubts. I am pulled to do what I know I shouldn't." I closed the book quickly. I didn't want to uncover Aunt Mary. Had she had temptations I knew nothing about? I held the book for a minute. She seemed unshakable. Had she been through the wilderness too?

I opened the book again. "I've reread Psalm 18 and will meditate on it. Surely I will get strength to go on." I thumbed through the following pages of the book. What had been her temptations? I couldn't find any and kept looking. Had she felt it unspoken, removing from me any chance of finding her humanity, and thus connecting me with her? She might have helped me understand she had been human too and a Christian despite her humanness.

"Why're you up there so long in the attic?" Jennifer called from the bottom of the steps.

*   *   *

A white bird flew in northern Missouri. A truck passed from McCormick's Distillery in Weston, Missouri, then Squaw Creek and on toward Kansas City. There was a cemetery on the hill, Afbay's and a turning cement truck.

In my distress I called upon the Lord, and cried unto my God; he heard my voice from his temple, and my cry came before him, even into his ears. Then the earth shook and trembled, the foundations of the world moved and were shaken. There went up a smoke out of his nostrils, and fire out of his mouth devoured; coals were kindled by it. He bowed the heavens also, and came down, and darkness was under his feet. The Lord thundered in the heavens, and the Highest gave his voice: hailstones and coals of fire. He sent from above; he took me, and drew me out of many waters. He delivered me from my enemies, for they were too strong for me. They came upon me in the day of my calamity, but the Lord was my stay. He brought me also into a large place, because he delighted in me—Psalm 18.

Eehaw

Heat waves on the highway into Leadville in the mule of a Missouri summer, stubborn with damp heat and rough as the coal bucket Pastor Hill rattled as he paced, preached.

We crossed the the Shoal creekbridge on Sunday, saw men fishing from the rail. "Just think," Aunt Mary would have said, "in church those fishers could be men."

The Journals

> Every man's words shall be his burden
> *Jeremiah 23:36*

I climbed Aunt Mary's attic in the heat. Thom and Jennifer played in the yard. Mother was on the porch swing.

We would clean out Aunt Mary's house. I wanted to save whatever Nealy would want. I was going to write to her about the journals I had found in the chest of drawers.

I opened the attic windows, but there was no breeze. I felt the dampness of my cotton dress already. The small attic was crowded with boxes and trunks and old furniture. In the corner I saw a small door. Maybe there was another part of the attic. Why hadn't Aunt Mary let us play up here when we were children?

He came when I wasn't expecting him. Aunt Mary had written.

> *Not in the least.*
> *I saw him cross the field on his camel.*
>
> *I made lemonade. He would be thirsty.*
> *We sat in the attic.*
> *He asked me to build a tabernacle*
> *where we could talk.*
> *Genesis was on his mind.*
>
> *The first day our Father made light.*
>
> *He divided from the dark.*
> *It was a light bulb he turned on in my head.*
> *A bulb I understood.*
> *He divided the old from the new.*

What could Aunt Mary have meant? I sat on the floor and read, drying the sweat with the hem of my dress.

> *There was a firmament in my head.*
> *A place not to drown.*
>
> *The waters gathered.*
> *Dry land appeared.*
>
> *In the heavens*
> *bunches of light.*

I fanned myself a moment with the journal. It was hard to breathe in the stuffy attic.

> *The fifth day the waters moved with fish.*
> *I felt them in my head.*
> *Whale.*
> *Minnow.*
> *Rock bass.*
> *Brook trout.*
> *Perch.*
> *Pike.*
> *Catfish.*

You see what's happening.

"Then drink your lemonade," I said.

I felt dizzy from the heat and closed the journal. I stood, my legs cramped under me, the dress stuck between my hips. I pulled it loose. Looked from the window. I heard Thom's voice around the corner. The porch swing squeaked. I opened the journal to another place.

> *Again.*
> *I feel it in my head.*
> *The waters trying to get loose.*
>
> *His voice.*
>
> *(The Fuller knows loneliness.*
> *He wants someone to talk to like us.)*

I lifted the hair from the back of my neck, and fanned it with the journal. Who came to see Aunt Mary? The Lord? Pastor Hill? I felt a chill in my back. Farley? What was I thinking?

> *He came wrapped in a blanket I didn't expect.*
> *He came in a form I wasn't familiar with.*

Not a graven image.
but his own.
I will look for the Indian blanket
Farley gave me
for the tabernacle curtain.

The Haul

On Saturday, dad and Farley came with the truck they borrowed from a neighbor. Aunt Mary's house seemed top heavy with the weight of the stuff in her attic. How did the house stay afloat? Mother and I had separated boxes of magazines and newspapers no one would want. We had another pile of old hats and dresses for a second-hand store in Hammergies. Pastor Hill took another load of hymnals and church stuff. I felt Aunt Mary's fishes move in my head. I sat on the sofa with my headache and listened to the screendoor wheeze as it opened and banged closed. I listened to the feet tromp across the porch. Was the Bible a state of mind? Light and dark, water and earth, establishing themselves? Making boundaries? Grasses blowing in the wind? Animals eating the grasses? Fishes in the deepest parts of themselves moving?

After lunch I went to the attic. Aunt Mary's journals were hidden in a drawer. I saw the path to the small attic door was cleared. We would be the rest of the summer going through her things.

Puncture Wounds

Gus had punctured the tires on the neighbor's Edsel. It took them a while to prove it. Until they found a scrap of cloth in their bushes that must have caught Gus's trousers. The tires were cut beyond recognition. But Gus had used Farley's fish-gutting knife. *The air was in the dark,* he said. He was only giving it some light.

November, in the *Chronicle's* Winnebago Brave

Farley and I were leaving Lawrence, Kansas, over the bridge before the turnpike—trees on the bend reflected in the Kaw like skeleton tribes that hunted the cement road and brown river.

Farley had been taking pictures of old Kansas cemeteries. I had been writing.

It must have been after they discovered fire that we passed, for we caught firebrands from their primeval dusk in the windshield.

The House

The paper boy threw the paper into the yard before he tied it with a string and the pages flew everywhere. I chased it across the yard and through the bushes in the blustery morning, returning to the dining room, which Thomas called the diving room, with the paper under my arm. I remembered great grandpa after his stock when they got loose from the pen.

I liked the old house in Kansas City where Thomas and I lived. The rooms were large and the ceiling high. There was a table for bread; chairs and a sofa around the fireplace. There was a bed in an empty room for mother when she fought with Bill. A kitchen wall for Farley's photographs.

Spinets

Hertess and Winifred Grostephan came from Hammergies for a visit.

"Have you seen my British Walkers?" Hertess asked her sister-in-law. "It's just as well," she said. "They're nothing more than my garden shoes now anyway."

"Medford had a weskit like that."

"You're not going to church here yet?"

"I can't fit into the printer's drawers."

"Well, at least you know the gospel."

"I've run from it all my life."

Winifred was Thomas's mother. Hertess, her husband's brother's wife. Both men were dead; Thomas's father for over twenty years and Hertess was a recent widow.

"Kansas City was platted on the south bank of the Missouri River in 1853." Hertess was a charter member of the Hammergies Historical Society. She also attended Kansas City's while they visited.

Winifred had taught third grade for years, saved all the children's papers which she asked to store in Aunt Mary's attic.

"I'm still cleaning out up there." I said. "Bring them to Kansas City. You can use my attic."

When Hertess's husband died, Winifred sold her house and moved into Hertess's small house in Hammergies. The women traveled when Winifred wasn't in school.

"The Cumberland Road connected at Wheeling with the Ohio River," Hertess always talked about history. "The Corders, Grostephans, and others, might have gone on, but Oregon was five months away. And by the spring thaw, they'd settled in Hammergies. Between 1843 and 1859, peak years in westward travel, one hundred thousand people passed along those trails."

"Mercy, Hertess," Winifred said.

"What trails?" I asked.

"Oregon, Sante Fe and California. Those were the three trails that left from Independence, Missouri, just east of Kansas City. Thirty thousand people died along the way."

Jennifer looked at Hertess and then to Winifred who washed the dishes while I rinsed the cornmeal and campfires from their conversation.

Updraft

Hertess and I drove her Peugeot into the University of Kansas City campus where a woman long ago rode a mule to the mill in the thaw of mud roads.

I waited by the rock wall in the cold sun for Hertess. She'd wanted to use the historical room of the library.

The cement walks had set in autumn. I saw the print of leaves, sediments from our urban civilization with those buried fossils of raftsmen and brush-burners.

Running, we crumble rock walls. The tudor and cement structures of the city university had been built on the soggy fields. The road upon which we traveled. Which way? Was not Rockets written upon his jacket as we passed?

History

A young wife came up the river with her husband and children, disembarked at Kansas City in the storm. A man with a lantern made his way through the boxes on the levee. The rain poured through Mrs. Corder's coat and print dress. They followed him to a riverfront mission. Some travelers were going across the Delaware Reserve into Kansas. Others were going north to the settlement of Hammergies. It was the first sermon many of them had heard since they arrived in Missouri, and *it spreads like smallpox*, the raftsman said.

Maybe a Start

Harsh lights came from the mouth of the cave. I had been left on open prairie, my belongings swept downstream. I held to Nealy's thought. There was a way. Faith was believing there was a God and that he would do what he said he would. The light at the cave hurt my eyes. I saw the windbreaks gone, the raw prairie, sod house, the newspapers stuffed in the cracks of the window.

Nealy Comes Back

Graveyard, briar patch. Nealy came home thin in a khaki dress and sandals, we sobbed together, her hair drawn back in a knot at the Kansas City airport.

Missouri River, jasper brown pavement reflected in the car window, brown as the river water that plowed by.

"We don't even have the same name, Hadley, Grostephan," she said, "and Jennifer."

"If you have to go somewhere else, why don't you preach on the reservations we have in America?"

Changed to Fish

Gus and Bill wrestled in the living room. But it wasn't wrestling. Gus had a girlfriend who laughed.

"Kill me—go ahead kill me," Gus had been drinking and let out a war-whoop.

Sometimes Gus gave us names. *Nealy-walks-on-water. Mother the child-eater.*

"We're all cannibals," Nealy said to Gus. "Didn't we eat Jesus in church?"

Bill-the-fish-chaser threw us to the water.

Which ate our feet. I'd always suspected the waves were teeth. Eating our legs and arms until we were only bodies like the fish. Wasn't that Bill and Ann's responsibility? Who knows how many arms and legs we'd once had.

The Wayfarers

From Kansas City, we went to Hammergies for a reunion with Pastor Hill. Nealy went to Aunt Mary's grave, then Farley came in his jeep. After the July Fourth, Farley took us to Minnesota through Iowa—past crumbling silo, old cement, the wires from underneath. Khaki also, the plains of Africa I saw in her, the stretches of country in Iowa on the way to Minnesota, bald river bluffs.

In Pawtucket, we waited for a train to cross the highway. Jennifer got in the front seat of the jeep beside Nealy. Thom and I were in the back. He hadn't wanted to come, kicked his foot against the seat until Farley told him to quit. Thomas worked and Bill was writing a series of articles. Mother wouldn't keep the children by herself. The wire in the cement of the crumbling silo stretched into telephone wires along the road, as I thought of my longing for Nealy. Farley was taking us to a church in Minnesota that supported Nealy's missionary work. There were eerie roads through fields, "a detour like Africa," Nealy said, "and the feeling of alone, Farley." He came too near a farmer's mailbox. Water holes. Broken trees. We passed Doon, Iowa, on K32. Swollen rivers and barren country.

"We're going farther west," I said.

"God knows the way."

9E then 75N again. Cement barn, at a broken corner the stone underneath. We had a canteen of water, windbreaks on the ground. "The highway is the Lord's," Nealy said as she talked of her missionary journeys. Jennifer slept against her shoulder.

Farley missed a turn and we came back south to highway 60E and traveled to Strobin, Minnesota, to the church that had given Nealy their offering, having lost a missionary of their own. We arrived in the evening. Jennifer and Thom were irritable and I had a headache from Farley's rough jeep. Nealy prayed for us and we slept at a widow's house.

Khaki stone church.

Nealy laughed when a child cried out as she

began to speak. Others came from New Ulm and Raphidan. Farley and Thom were at the river.

"The children cried out there too," she said. "So it is in the spirit. A soul separated unto God is a spectacle. It goes to church, prays to someone it cannot see. It has faith in that which is against reason. It walks in a land the unbeliever cannot know. 'Thou will be my map, the Lord my God will light my darkness—' Psalm 18:28."

Nealy preached at another church in Minnesota. Farley fished the creeks, and we started back to Hammergies. Nealy was crying to be said, a light in a dark land. And so it is, strung wire to wire, we crossed the country, pilgrims and sojourners. "Jesus rode on an ass into Jerusalem, his own will bridled. Jesus my redeemer and strength."

"You never stray, Nealy," I said as Farley drove us back to Missouri.

"What else is there, Hadley?"

I thought of my own barren life. "Nothing, Nealy."

"You're running after the donkey like Saul, instead of riding," Nealy said.

Farley laughed.

He stopped as we came back through Pawtucket, Iowa, and got out of the jeep with his cameras. "You've got an eye for God's creation, Farley," Nealy said. "Don't you ever see the creator in it?"

"I see what's there, Miss Williges," Farley told her, "not what isn't."

"You're on earth to prepare to meet your Lord. You live in darkness, Farley."

"What do you want, lady?" I heard anger in Farley's voice.

"I want you to accept Jesus Christ as your Savior and Lord."

"Don't believe in it."

"Farley, it's you who's separated from God. I won't always be with you. If you die like you are, you're left out of the heaven in God's Bible."

Farley looked down the road. I would have left him alone, he'd been pricked often enough. I walked along the ditch with Thom and gathered weeds and cornflowers, looking now and then at the wide Iowa sky. Jennifer had been asleep in the jeep. She was awake now, came and pulled weeds with us, clots of dirt hanging from the stalks. Farley and Nealy talked at the jeep.

I had a different road than Nealy. She was

always close to God. Lived in the adjacent room. He called her to be a missionary when they talked at the table over their toast and ham. But God had called me too, even me, with a holy calling. Hadley Grostephan in the duststorm, bumpy road, with headaches, heatwaves in the Iowa field, uncertain way. But a highway was there, and a way. And it was for the wayfaring—Isaiah 35:8.

Nealy in Cornflowers in Pawtucket

"The lines of his pipe are in the fencepost and broken rail," Nealy said of Farley, "his thoughts like smoke."

She stood in cornflowers in a blue print dress and sandals, her hair tied back.

Pawtucket and cornflowers in Farley's camera.

"If you'll give yourself to the Lord," Nealy still spoke to Farley until he walked away.

"When will you believe God?" She called after him.

"When I can take a photograph of him."

"I'll send your camera with you when you die."

Farley looked back at her.

"Now, Farley, you're a fisherman." Nealy continued her assault when he walked near us again. "There're your bottom feeders like the catfish. They eat by smell. Their nose always in the bottom of the creek. Sucking up the silt, eating mud, spitting out the rest. You take your stinky bait and stand at the creek for them.

"But then there's bass. Always looking up. That's why their eyes are big as a catfish's whiskers. You take your spinner and go get them."

Farley walked off again.

Barbed-wire and smoke, old bark.

A limb cracked by lightning-bolts.

"It comes back, Nealy," I said—"the washboard years." And we cried at Farley's pipe-rail fence.

The Bus Stop in Nigeria

We came back to Hammergies, stayed in Aunt Mary's house. Nealy preached at the Hammergies Church and Farley went back to Kansas City. Thomas would come for us later, after Thom went to scout camp.

"I thought I'd keep the house for you, Nealy," mother said. She'd lived in it awhile after Aunt Mary's death, then returned to dad. "Surely you won't be in Africa forever. I couldn't stand it for it to belong to another family; it's the Corder house."

"I won't be back for a long time, mother."

"Vandals break the windows when we're not here," I said. "It can't sit vacant either."

"I wish I knew what to do," mother said.

We talked awhile longer and decided to rent the house.

Nealy had another church to visit and I wanted to drive Aunt Mary's old DeSoto.

"I think I'd rather ride the bus, Hadley," Nealy said.

I looked at her.

"In places in Nigeria," she said, "we gather at the bus stop," C.C. was there then too, Caroline Catherine McGreevy, her hair graying. "And when there's enough people, the bus leaves. They bring their bedding, their chickens, sometimes we wait days."

"Nealy," C.C. said, shaking her head.

"I want a bus schedule in my hand, and I want to be on the 4:05 when it leaves at 4:05."

The Tabernacle

Nealy and I spent the day in Aunt Mary's attic. I looked through the last of the trunks and boxes. Nealy sat in the corner reading Aunt Mary's journals.

"All these sermons she wrote—" Nealy thumbed through another journal.

"Why didn't Pastor Hill let her preach now and then?" I asked angrily.

"Here's her prayer for the *Chronicle* to revive after we moved to Indiana. Here's her prayers for us."

I'd given up on the journals. Aunt Mary's handwriting was hard to read. Often I didn't know what she meant.

"Holy Moly," Nealy said. "Anna Ruth was impaled on a picket fence. Mary and her older sister had been playing angels. Trying to walk on the fence when Anna Ruth fell. Aunt Mary's sister, Hadley, was crucified on a fence. Mary Corder gave herself to God because of it. It was Anna Ruth's death that sent Aunt Mary into God's arms."

I knelt by Nealy as she read.

What had that meant to mother? She had been born many years later, with nearly the same name. Was part of her rage a ghost voice of Anna Ruth?

*   *   *

Clinter Krudup drove by in his truck several times near dark before he stopped. "What're you doing with Mary Corder's house?" He looked at Nealy as we carried a box to the curb for the trash man.

"We're keeping it, Clinter," I told him. "Maybe we'll rent it."

"But where would we stay July Fourth?" Nealy asked.

"We just have to get rid of some of Aunt Mary's belongings."

"Want me to carry anything?"

"We've got a door in the attic we haven't opened yet—"

"Might drive by again."

Nealy pushed open the small door in Aunt Mary's attic. Inside was a course, heavy curtain. Nealy pushed it back. The bright sun in the east attic window made us squint.

Inside the heavy blanket, I saw another blanket, striped black, white and red. "It's the blanket Farley brought her—remember Nealy? From the Pottawatomie Reservation. I thought she threw it away, but I read about it in her journal—"

"I thought there would be more boxes and trunks. I think Aunt Mary saved everything the family owned." Nealy looked behind the Indian blanket. There was a large, trunk-like box.

"Aunt Mary made this?" I said, looking at it.

"Don't touch it, Hadley." Nealy said.

I drew back.

"Why?"

Nealy looked at the trunk. "The ark of the covenant." She turned quickly. "The altar of incense. The candlestick. The table—My Lord, Hadley, this is the tabernacle in the wilderness."

"The what—"

"Look, Hadley, inside this first blanket, the brazen altar and laver. Then under Farley's blanket the three pieces of furniture inside the tabernacle tent, then the ark of the covenant in the Holy of Holies."

"What is that?"

"The mercy seat over the ark of the covenant. Hadley," Nealy took my arm. "Aunt Mary had the tabernacle hidden in her attic. This must be where she came to pray. And to give those sermons I read in her journals. It was the Old Testament church for Israel. Only in those days they couldn't enter like we do. Only the priests. The brazen altar is where the people brought their bulls and goats and rams to sacrifice.

"Aunt Mary's journals are the sermons she must have given. No one would let her talk in church. She gave them to the attic. To the congregation of dust and spiders. Of the top of the trees. The birds who passed there. The planes somewhere far up in the sky."

"How do you know?"

"Because I do. The blankets, the laver, the candlestick. It's all here, Hadley. The brazen altar and a laver. Our burnt offering and washing in the courtyard. Then the holy place in the tent. 'I will meet with you and talk with you from above the mercy seat and between the two cherubim which are upon the ark of the covenant.'"

"It's like the tent grounds when the carnival first comes to town. The balloon woman sells tickets—while her black balloons beat the wind."

"Look at the spots on the floor, Hadley. Aunt Mary must have sacrificed too."

I looked closely at the floor. Nealy looked around the brazen altar. She lifted the grill. She let the lid fall back down.

Nealy turned pale.

What?—" I asked.

I looked inside. Small bones. Bird bones. Aunt Mary must have sacrificed birds. "Those are blood-spots on the floor, Nealy," I said. "How'd she trap them?"

"Somehow she did," Nealy answered. "She sacrificed the birds at the altar. Aunt Mary did more than write sermons and preach up here—"

Nealy backed from the tabernacle in the wilderness, bumped her head on the small attic door, ran through the attic and down the stairs. I burst after her, but she was out of the house and far down the street. I heard a truck brake and turn in a whirl. Clinter Krudup would reach her first.

I heard Nealy's scream as I ran to hold her.

"She had it wrong, Hadley," Nealy said when she could talk. "The sacrifices are over. Christ put an end to it all—" Nealy's voice broke and she sobbed in Clinter and my arms.

Fire

Nealy pulled down the blankets from the attic. Clinter carried the ark of the covenant, the altar of incense—everything to the backyard incinerator. Nealy broke up the pieces of furniture and put them in the fire. "It is finished," she said.

The Farewell

"I want to come to Africa someday, Nealy," I cried as she packed after several months in Kansas City. "I could bring the children—"

"It's too rough for them, Hadley." Nealy said. "The climate—the difference in culture—"

"You went."

"I was called. I didn't go for a visit. The angels went with me."

"But Nealy—"

"Those women squatting over the cooking fires—the huts—the fevers—"

I looked at her.

"The noises in the night. Is that for you, Hadley?"

"Is it for you?"

At the Kansas City Airport

I cried at the airport when Nealy left because I felt my aloneness on the earth without her. "Why is there suffering?" I asked.

"Because there is," she answered.

"Nealy, it's like the time we had mumps and chickenpox together and mother had them too. And you and I stayed together in our room you sucked my hair until it was long strands of an African river."

After Nealy Left

At first it was a small place like the apartment we had in Indiana long ago when the *Chronicle* folded for a while with a Murphy bed which came down from the wall when Nealy and I slept and raised again when we woke.

Thomas struggled with the small law firm

he had formed with two other partners, was often grouchy when he came for supper.

I didn't want to cook or do housework. I only waited for the time to pass. I wanted to be on the road with Farley. I wanted to write.

Gus finally married the girl he had been living with. They moved to Hammergies to start again in Aunt Mary's house. And how would we divide Beethoven, I thought at their wedding, should Thomas and I separate?

Nasturtium and Sweetpea

In the dark days after Nealy left, I attended a church in Kansas City. Nealy'd been my friend. There wasn't anyone else. I didn't want to go to the church I'd gone to as a girl in Kansas City. I couldn't really say what the pastor preached. I couldn't run to Hammergies every time I went to church.

Well, Farley played the saw, a jagged high-pitched whine, felt like lightning-bolts from God— hail and thunder flashes. Aunt Mary's instrument had been the ragged edge of her tongue. "They made the gospel bitter," I told Pastor Reams at the church where I took the children in Kansas City.

Nazareth was a harsh place too. "It was a long war between the house of Saul and the house of David," Reams preached, "but David grew stronger and the house of Saul weaker, II Samuel 3:1."

I went to church Sunday morning, Sunday night, then Wednesday night and the women had a prayer meeting. Bill and Ann's house could buck with turmoil. Mine could feel like a cleaned-out attic. But church was solid. It was there. Gus was in a rehabilitation program. I felt like our words could hold him on line. My car, like Aunt Mary's DeSoto, could hardly pass a church.

> Once there, it wasn't as bad
> as we thought.
>
> *James Tate*
> "The Tabernacle"

We began church at the altar—winter sun through the window, round as the flue-cover on the kitchen wall and the thicket's haze in holy glory. We prayed at the altar, raised our hands—the wind hard as knees on the wooden floor that ripped through windbreaks, topsoil, into the hailstone's holy light.

Tractor Pull

Gus had started Grandpa Corder's tractor Aunt Mary kept. It bucked through the far end of her garage and over the field behind her house. Bill went running after him. Mother screaming, *get him, get him*. Farley yelling, *go buckeroo*.

Reading

In winter the old tree in the yard caught clouds and sturgeon on blustery days. And jagged branches made shadows on the ground like tenuous roads where we had passed.

Farley was in our yard all afternoon taking pictures of the shadows on the ground and branches like fishnet where he, too, was caught.

After a while he came to the door. "What'ya doin'?"

"I'm looking at a book before Thom and Jenny get home from school. I have all these books I've never read. My own words get in the way, I guess. I'd rather be writing. But I'd know so much more if I read."

Farley sat in the kitchen talking about Bill and Ann.

"What keeps them from splitting?" I asked. "We're grown. Why do they stay together?"

"They love one another, Hadley."

"More than Thomas and I who don't have the arguments, the anger and violence."

Where does that love come from? That commitment that holds, no matter what happens. It was the love Nealy felt for God.

"I've read the Bible, Hadley." Farley looked at me with his own news. "Something you and Miss Nealy don't know. I was struck how God knew the names of his people. He counted them all. But he seems cranky more often than not. If you didn't please him, it is sword, famine, pestilence, death. 'I will utterly forget you'—Jeremiah 23:39. Yes, that's our God."

We talked until Thom and Jennifer came in the

door. Jennifer ran to Farley's lap. Thom opened the fridge door looking for milk.

Squirrels

We had squirrels in the attic. Thomas was trapping them one Saturday when Farley came by. The children were in the den watching television. They hardly looked up from their program.

Did I want to go with him? He asked on his way from town. He would even dump our squirrels in the country if I would go. But Thomas hadn't caught them yet.

I had started half-days at the *Chronicle*, returning to the house before the children were back from school. Sometimes I covered religious councils and church meetings with Juan Piccola, the atheist religious editor. But I wanted to be on the editorial page.

"Now there is suffering for the Christian, Hadley," Nealy wrote. I was reading her letter when Farley came. He took it from me to read.

"You need a ride," Farley said.

Jennifer called after us to wait.

I was bored with work and the family. Traveling with Farley, I began to see the country again.

He stopped to take a picture of the late sky where the sun came down through the clouds in long cornfield-rows.

Jennifer shivered in the jeep and called for us to hurry.

"Why do you go to church?" Farley asked as we drove again.

"Nealy's gone. I need something to hang on to."

Farley took several pages of pictures for the Sunday paper that afternoon in the country. Gasoline was scarce, and people couldn't afford it anyway. Farley did a *Sunday Ride* section in the *Chronicle* for people who couldn't get away from Kansas City.

The Let-Down

I wanted to be on the editorial page. But Hertha Jollet beat me out. "You haven't paid your dues, Hadley," Bill said.

"I have with you," I answered.

I went to the religious page instead.

*   *   *

"God's army is conscript—" I talked to Edward Macs, a black minister in Kansas City, whose church had burned. "Why me and not the next one?"

I had taken a week off work, while the children were on a break from school. "Why do I hear God's voice like a sergeant and when others don't hear at all?"

I was supposed to be asking Edward Macs about his church, but instead we talked about faith—and being Christians, how we were pressed into a different place, which others didn't see, a place from which I had fallen once and returned, but felt pulled away from again, though I wouldn't go far. "At least I won't do what I want to."

"And what's that?"

"I want to be like Farley, my uncle, the photographer at the *Chronicle*. He takes pleasure in what he does. It fits him, anyway. And probably me too, if I would let it."

"And you think the Christian doesn't get what he wants? But always has to do what he doesn't?"

"No. I have a sister who is a missionary in Africa and she's satisfied, like Farley."

He asked me more about Nealy.

"But there's a discrepancy between what I want and what I do," I said, getting back to our first conversation. "I guess Christianity for me is not getting to do what I want. I want to work at the *Chronicle*, but I have the burden of husband and children—and my mother, who is sometimes at my house before I get home from work, waiting to rage about my father. I don't always want to be there for the children. I want to go off with Farley and not come back until I remember my way home. On Sunday mornings, I want to sleep late, but the minister expects me to teach a Sunday school class. It's not that I want to do anything wrong—it's just that I feel trapped. I don't want all the rules of church. I keep hoping Christ will be something more."

I talked a while longer in Edward Macs' office in the rectory. Outside, the charred remains of his church.

"Yet I don't want to be like Farley," I told him. "He doesn't know God unless he sees him in his camera lens. How sorry he will be when he sees heaven. What he could have had. The cameras— The landscapes waiting for him there. I guess Nealy is who I'd like to be like. I want to have pleasure in doing what I know to do."

Macs laughed. We had uncovered ourselves. I forgot the article I was supposed to write and apologized to Edward Macs. I asked again about the fire.

"When I have trouble with myself," he said, "I think of the Lord before his disciples when he had to say, 'How long will I be with you? How long will I suffer you?' That's me talking to myself." Macs said. "I can see the Lord speaking to his disciples with his hand on the back of his neck—stiff, the way mine sometimes gets."

"And mine. I think that's the reason for my headaches some of the time."

I wrote an article for the *Chronicle* on Edward Macs and the congregation coping with their loss and rebuilding and I wrote about the struggle of faith. It was unorthodox, in that it talked about the cleft between faith and experience. How we have to approach God creatively to make the relationship work. It would upset ministers, but it went directly to the point of fissure in me.

"Hadley Williges?" Thomas questioned the by-line.

"Hadley Williges Grostephan won't fit on a newspaper column."

"Shorten it to Hadley Grostephan."

I got more letters on Edward Macs than on anything I had done for the *Chronicle*.

The Argument

"If I could work full-time," I said to Thomas, "I could probably be editor of the religious page, or the feature section." I had another letter from the Edward Macs article on the table—*Better than that heathen you got working on the religious page.* We'd always had complaints about Juan Piccola.

"I want you here when the children come home from school," Thomas said. It was the same argument we always had. "You don't have to work," he went on. "I don't want you around Farley all the time either," he said. Mother agreed with that.

"After working all these years at the *Chronicle*, the editor finally wants me as a newsperson and not Bill's daughter. I can't ignore that."

Pescado

Farley went to Mexico in his chino pants, a new dinghy tied on top of his Datsun, his camera and lenses on the seat beside him.

"Jesus," mother said.

"Just think where you could be going," he said to me as he left.

We didn't hear from him for a month.

Then one morning, when I came downstairs, he and Thomas were at the breakfast table with Farley's pictures.

"Hola," Farley said. I looked to see if he had met the barbed iron and fish spears mother and Aunt Mary had threatened—

"Back to Flat Creek and Mussel Fork?" I asked.

He brought Jennifer a fish piñata. "Pescado means fish, but a fish that has been caught. There's a difference, Hadley," he took his pipe from his mouth.

"We've been waiting years for you to make that discovery."

"There's another word for the fish still in the water."

Thomas had to go to the office on Saturday, and left Farley and me in the middle of the river.

"Epictetus spoke of volition." Farley said.

"So did Cain. But I am willing to be a caught-fish on the string of The Fisherman, while you remain in the water. What's the word, Farley, for a fish with a mind of its own?"

"Hadley Williges, I guess," he said.

"Mrs. Grostephan to you," I answered. "I've been gathered from the waters—saved, Farley—and that Christ life in me is stronger than anything that could pull me back into the water."

Olé," he said, as he left with his pictures.

Survival

Bill said he was afraid the *Chronicle* would fold.

"It happened once before," mother said when they came to supper at our house.

"Farley's been asked to work at the *Star*."

"But he wouldn't leave you, would he, Bill?" Mother looked at him. "No, there's not a chance."

"Farley's worked for the *Chronicle* all his life."

"It was Bill who got him the job," mother said.

"Farley wouldn't leave the *Chronicle*," Thomas said.

I knew Farley'd stayed boarded up in our house with his *tuba* while we went to Indiana when the *Chronicle* folded once before. But we'd come back to Kansas City and Farley and his *tuba* moved out. I remembered when Farley'd wanted to be a musician. Sometimes I could hear his pictures.

Farley fiddled with the edge of a photograph in the editorial meeting the next afternoon.

"What can we give the readers the other papers don't?" Mr. Creveling, the owner and editor, looked at us. Around him sat Gramilla, Juan Piccola, Hertha Jollet, Margaret Crussel of the Obituaries, Farley, Bill, assorted others and myself.

"Culture."

"A sense of ourselves," we answered Mr. Creveling's question.

"The Missouri landscape of Farley's pictures."

"Texture." Everyone looked at me. "A ship going in several directions yet on course." I made my remarks more obtuse.

"Tradition, yet risk."

"Editorials."

Cabool, Missouri

I was in southern Missouri with Farley where a long trail of Cherokee had passed. Over a hundred and fifty years ago. I stopped by the road while I waited for Farley to get out of bed. Once in a while I could hear their voices.

The baby has no one to feed it. Leave it by the farmer's road. Move on. Keep walking.

We camped around dusk. The whole train fell to the ground, some sleeping before they ate. Several in the party died that night. Some disappeared.

Another Trip with Farley

The farmer ploughs into the ground the plough, the oxen, his body, the window of his voorhuis and the windmill above the borehold.

It was raining that morning we drove through Joplin. The gates of Farley's windshield wipers blowing closed and open. I saw a church I knew preached the gospel, but couldn't get to it from the interstate and we spent that Sunday driving to Kansas City in the rain.

Boaz

The next week Jennifer and I drove north along the old River Road toward Hammergies. We were going to have lunch with Hertess and Winifred Grostephan. We passed fields in rows of broken cornstalks. The rock ledges stacked like plates along the road by the Missouri River. Snow from the late storm was still on the fields.

It was Anna Ruth and Aunt Mary who had gleaned fields and threshing floors from Moab to Judah. As girls, they had stacked the plates of rock in river bluffs. But walking on the fence-top, Anna Ruth had caught her foot, or the hem of her dress, on the sharp picket fence.

Her fingers had been like chalk in a box.

Aunt Mary wanted to preach. Take Jeremiah and Zebediah between her teeth. Tell the burden of words to leap from her mouth into the ears of her congregation. Where they sat all whoperjawed and kinked. Stuck in the small town while the whole world twinked around the sun. She had wanted to talk to humanity full of hurt and hurting. Nothing but the cross would ever set them straight. But Aunt

Mary didn't preach—except in her attic behind the small door where she kept the altar of blood, and sacrificed little field-mice and birds at the brazen altar of the Old Testament tabernacle—and entered the Holy of Holies where the Shekinah glory shone between the cherubim.

Aunt Mary'd held church in her attic.

And over the white creeks and fields of Missouri late in March, the carp were as full of bones as the snow.

The Letter

Nealy was coming back to America. She needed a rest. Africa wore on her, she wrote, and as yet she couldn't always endure it.

"—I'm beginning to find my style. Stories come, Farley," I said, "like fields along the road."

Kansas City had reached eight hundred thousand in population and Mr. Creveling, the editor, was changing the format of the *Chronicle* in a last attempt to keep the paper alive.

"The eight hundred thousand must include the

crows flying over," Farley said and took a picture of a flock of birds for the paper.

Hertha Jollet and others resented the fact that I could work half-days at the *Chronicle* and not come in at all if Thom or Jennifer were sick. Yet I received bylines and got the stories Bill and sometimes Farley found.

The Missionary

"She was born in a wagon," Gus said. In journeying often, she crossed the Atlantic four times, quinine from northern Missouri for malaria and snowshoes for the Nigerian sun. She drove into the mountains of Uzebba with her interpreter, she told the congregation at Edward Macs' church where we visited. She preached, and baptized converts. Then she went onto Mushin, Owo. On a dusty road, a chief wanted to accept the salvation he'd heard of for his tribe, and hearing each one had to do it on his/her own, he turned back into the brush.

"We come to Jesus Christ as individuals," Nealy

preached at Emure-Ekiti and thirsted so herself, she drank boiled water while it was yet hot.

Through the years she prayed into the burning winds, native revolts, and read her testament to the perils in the wilderness. He said to the snow, Be thou on earth—Job 37:6. By the breath of God frost is given, as wagon wheels moved through the heat in her bones.

The Cornwallis

Mother and I decided we'd stay in Kansas City for the Fourth. I'd been to the Hammergies Reune since I was born. But Nealy insisted—and for some reason, Farley felt patriotic. The Hammergies Reune meant something to him, he said. "Let's go just for the day."

Nealy and I looked at each other. "Is that Farley Williges?" We asked.

Mr. Creveling said he was tired of it also—didn't want small-town news in the *Chronicle*. Didn't know if the *Chronicle* would last past the Fourth anyway. We had enough happening in Kansas City without reporting Hammergies.

Nevertheless, Farley took us to the July Fourth in Hammergies—though it took two cars for Bill, Farley and mother, Nealy, Thom, Thomas, Jennifer and me.

We stayed in Aunt Mary's house where Gus and his wife lived—who were going to have a child.

We drove into the yard of Aunt Mary's house on the wide lot Gus mowed in the summer. Farley parked under the large trees hovering like helicopters.

"I have dreams of crucified birds," Gus said. "Their wings spread as if nailed to a cross. Their blood dripping into the rainspout."

"There's no such thing," mother said.

"I haven't heard of it either," Gus's wife agreed.

There were foot races at the Hammergies Church for the July Fourth, then Pastor Hill, his nephew and sons, read David's Psalms while Nealy played the flute and Farley the saw.

Thom and Jennifer went off with mother to the new rides.

Nealy talked with Farley on the edge of the highway where the cars were parked. *Isaiah and Ahaz in the conduit of the fuller's field,* I thought, as prophet gave counsel to king. Farley was in trouble at the *Chronicle,* the traffic bureau and mother.

I saw Horace Krudup, C.C. McGreevy, and talked to her. Jason was no longer her husband, but someone else. Clinter still looked at Nealy.

When Rezin and Pekah came to Jerusalem to war, Isaiah told Ahaz, *be not fainthearted, for the tails of those smoking firebrands would not stand*—Isaiah 7:4,7 Pastor Hill preached over the loud speaker.

But if Ahaz didn't believe, surely he would not be established.

I heard Thom call.

At night, the fireworks and bonfire. And at night, the battle for the end of the conduit in the highway of the fuller's field, when Rezin of Syria and Pekah of Ahaz's own divided people came, not as armies, but abstractions through the apertures in our garrison. And what we hold onto is ours—

Toe Hold

Gus had stuck fire-crackers in the angels he made. *Pissing from heaven*, Gus called the angels exploding behind the tent-revival.

But inside, the noise of heaven was what you thought you heard.

Crowds came for prayer.

The long-line backed.

Anencephalous. The woman's baby born without a brain, its forehead sloping from its eyebrows to the brainstem. *That's what we're without rebirth*, Pastor Hill poked. *The blood-bath of Jesus.* Our spirit's all collapsed, can't pass through the fine-meshed-fence of heaven. A crumpled balloon. Only a face without the back of the head. The engine room.

The boy who couldn't spell was next. *Geece. Geace. Giese. Geuze. Gieze.* He never spelled the same way twice. His teacher read his papers as if she swallowed needles. The Lord greasing her throat with Crisco first.

The stars were former lights. Hallo-loo-yah. Pastor Hill was known for saying. Without Jesus we're the stars and moon without the sun.

Aunt Mary had flipped. She knew the angel making messes.

Inside Jesus punched the hollow-sack of our heart. It was night in there if He hadn't filled our black sky with tiny explosions. Pastor Hill was saying we had wire-cutters for feet. *See the bloody prints behind us where we been. See the fence we cut with prayer?* He used his pointer. None of us could be freed of our bonds any better. No none. Now close your barn door. Get a toe-hold.

Hertha Jollet

Red barn, truss bridge, tall row of weeds, plowed field.

Photography was the likeness of what Farley saw in relationship to what he was—in reference to his inward frame.

I waited outside the darkroom with Hertha for pictures to our separate stories.

Mr. Creveling went into his office.

"I hear discord in the wind." I said of my discontent as Farley worked. "—and my wagon without wheels."

"I don't hear it that way," she said.

"There're many voices. We hear what we hear."

Farley came from the darkroom and handed us our pictures.

"My sweet tuba," I heard him say.

A Puzzle Piece

I was waiting for Thomas to come from his law office. We'd meet for a concert and late supper. We'd been married nearly fifteen years. When I saw Farley and Hertha leave.

The Plainsman

Because I didn't go when they made their way across the west, but stayed in Missouri, and that, of late, and even when Gus wrote back from Oregon in his mind, I left the wagons unhitched.

It was a month before the letter came and Oregon was months away. Not many returned, I noticed, the same as when they left. And I took the vision of Daniel, Ezekiel, and John, of the days upon us, and in those days to come, Oregon was not any place to be.

The Missionary Returns

Nealy sat in her granny glasses writing to Clarence at the mission in Oshodi in Nigeria, West Africa. She had her black testament open as she wrote. Her slight hooked nose gave a nasal sound to her voice as she hummed. She'd caught a cold as the year moved into winter.

"What does a woman like you do in Africa?" a man asked her at the Wednesday night meeting at church.

"Nearly the same thing I do here," she answered. "I preach. The Lord converts souls. The word stalks their drums, and wind takes the gospel among their cooking pots and spears. We travel toward healing. Toward civilization."

"Those two are the same?" he asked.

He was a handsome man. His hair brown with gray in it. He was proud. He dismissed me as uninteresting at a glance, made me self-conscious, affirming the awkwardness I felt.

*   *   *

Nealy's flute played in the morning. Thomas complained. "I get tired of it too," I said. "But we rented Aunt Mary's house in Hammergies."

Columns like silos, windmills, the ceiling like a gage.

"You should have been a musician, Nealy—"

The morning squeaked like Nealy's flute.

I got the children off to school.

The Old Airport

It was the small house where we had grown up. Nealy talked to mother in the kitchen. I sat in the living room looking at the chair. The mock-orange bush was in the backyard, the woodpile and the four o'clocks by the backsteps folding every afternoon like mother. It was one of those houses, narrow in width, but it had length. A living room was across the front of the house, the kitchen and dining room, side by side, came next. Then the two small bedrooms in back where Bill and Ann slept. Upstairs, Gus, Nealy and I had our rooms.

At night Nealy and I had blown into a black

balloon that filled our hollow room, so the blackness of open space wouldn't collapse on us. But when it did, we could hear Gus in his room making plane-engine noise with his throat. We could hear him flying over, circling back for us, his feet on the throttle, his hands on the wheel. Lifting us slowly from the house. Our heads pulled back.

The Preacher

"Thomas is the head of the house."

"Don't start, Nealy."

"Which of you goes to church?"

"Me."

"Then you have the greater responsibility to obey God."

"I don't like rules. I want to see Christ as a reporter for the *Chronicle*. Or Christ as story, the telling of many words. Not all agreeing with one another. With room. ROOM, Nealy, to move."

"Then you don't know the God I do."

"How dare you fly in here from the sandhills and sawmills of some ancient village and tell me what to do."

"It's the same in the city, Hadley."

"You're heavy, Jennifer," I said, "get off my lap. Go read your book."

She was almost as big as we were.

Nealy sat at my kitchen table studying Farley's pictures and giving me scriptures. Thom and his father were at a scout meeting. Thom was going to work at Camp Osceola as a counselor in the summer.

Nealy and I cried. "There's nothing, Nealy. Thomas and I aren't close. I'm bored with my marriage, but I hold steady, unlike Bill and Ann. My children haven't heard anything like we did." I blew my nose in one of Farley's handkerchiefs I had in my pocket. "I can't do what Thomas wants. He wants me to stay here and look at the four walls."

"He might want what's best for the family."

"I'd turn into mother in my frustration."

"If you don't jump in demanding what you want, maybe God will change Thomas's mind."

"Marriage to Thomas was something I did before I came to myself."

"Well, now you have yourself, you can do what God would have asked you do in the beginning."

"And what's that?" I asked. "Stay with Thomas when I don't want to?"

"Yes."

"Nobody would agree with you."

"God would."

I looked at her angrily. "What do you know? You went to some Bible school and they sent you off someplace I've never heard of because they didn't know what else to do with you, and you come back with all the answers you think I need from your narrow life. I don't have any feelings for the marriage."

"Marriage is an agreement to work together," Nealy kept on. "It's a decision. What does it have to do with feeling?"

Even Great-Grandpa Corder Knew That

In the Carolinas, great-grandma Corder had a three-story house, one-room-narrow, and straight-up. The staircase was wide enough for great-grandma with her oil lamp, and great-grandpa with his arms at his sides. They brought a picture of the house with them to Missouri. I found it in Aunt Mary's belongings in the attic. A bureau was lowered with ropes through a window when they moved.

Also their small table, the beds and great-grandpa
carrying a cradle. The floors sloped like a soup bowl.
They came to Missouri looking for flat space.

Drought

The floors creaked, and the stairs. I'd been
afraid to go downstairs in the dark, always afraid I'd
hear angry voices from the night. But the Lord had
lightened my darkness and I went down, choked
with sobs again as I thought of my empty life with
Thomas. Only the Lord could plough the barren
fields we passed. I prayed at the window seat in the
living room. It was on the north, I realized, and cried
again. I begged for a finish to the marriage, that I
could ask Thomas to leave. Hadn't it ended anyway?
I begged for the *Chronicle* to continue though I knew
it couldn't. I begged for Farley who was going somewhere far away.

The prayers in the night lasted for months.
Nealy came and went, traveled to Bynumville, Boswell—and churches Aunt Mary used to visit—for
support of her mission. Sometimes I went and some-

times I stayed in Kansas City with Thomas and the children.

"How long will you be here?" I asked Nealy again.

"I've got to stay the winter, feel the snow again," Nealy answered.

"And Nealy," I said, "aren't you running like me? You've refused a family and ride your bike around Africa. Did you come out so much better?"

The Christening

Will you play with him as a bird?
Job 41:5

Gus and his wife had their child christened in Hammergies, just as Thom and Jennifer were. Gus had accepted the Lord as his savior, but he could stay away from church, unlike me. Nevertheless, he wanted his child christened.

We all stood with them at the altar, while Pastor Hill held the child. Farley, mother, Bill, Nealy, Thomas, the children and I. Even Hertess and Winifred Grostephan came.

Sometimes I thought I heard bird-noises. Or

saw something fly in the arm of the cross-shaped church. Once I looked at Gus. But I thought it was from outside.

He still had dreams of birds with their wings nailed outspread. He'd pulled down the fences in Aunt Mary's backyard.

"They aren't there, Gus," his wife had looked at the heap.

"The birds were in the attic, Gus," Nealy'd told him. "Aunt Mary kept an altar and made sacrifices for us."

But Gus thought birds were in the church. He hit the air as if the birds were there. Mother must have been afraid he'd beat the walls. She rushed at him. Bill rushed at her.

Gus hit harder, sweeping his arms over them. Mother screamed. Gus's wife teetered up and down. Hertess and Winifred stood in horror. Thomas held the children.

Farley, Nealy and I held Gus down while mother got away.

"We're in Christ, Gus," I said. "We can hold still when the world is flying."

I could hear Jennifer calling me. The baby crying. Farley's head nodding like a bobber on Flat Creek.

The Circuit

Blackened fields, birds in the pews of trees, windbreaks and brushfires on the edge of towns we circulated. Boswell, DeWitt, Rensselaer, Polo, Perry—dispatched their fire and brimstone sermons.

I worked for the religious page during the last days of the paper. Unburdened with my passion for everything. Maybe that numbness was what Farley always had. But his numbness was for the world and the human condition. Just driving through. Getting shaken now and then. Taking a few pictures. Making a few words.

The Headaches Speak

An evangelist came through Kansas City. I covered his revival for the *Chronicle*. It would be my last story. Nealy, Bill and Ann came with me. Farley was in the backdrop taking pictures. The armory was crowded with people. Pastor Reams, Edward Macs, other ministers I knew, were seated on the platform.

Even Pastor Hill had come from Hammergies. He'd met the evangelist years ago.

Hertess and Winifred Grostephan had ridden with him, but they stayed at the house with Thomas and the children.

One of the ministers came to the pulpit on the edge of the stage in the armory. He raised his hands and prayed. A hum of prayer went up around the armory. The minister called the gospel singers. They sang. Then another minister prayed. The hum of voices went up again in the armory. The minister prayed for the sick. The despondent. The hungry. Diseased. Famined. Deathed. Surely the conflicts and suffering in the world pointed to the end of days when the Lord returned.

The minister finished praying, then called the evangelist, who came to the pulpit with his arms raised. "Are you saved?" he asked. The crowd in the armory roared. The gospel choir jumped. Their robes rippled like a wall of curtains shaken out.

The evangelist preached. *Turn in your Bibles to the book of Isaiah*—

In the armory, Jesus was a spirit and not a denomination. He was a high flyer. I remembered Aunt Mary on her way to a revival in a country church when she hit some chickens along the road, splattering one across our windshield. Nealy and I had screamed. "We're a bloody race," Mary snorted in her ecstasy and raced on toward church.

Yes, Jesus was here and he was there—in the rows behind me. In the rows beside. He was in the here and now. He was in the hereafter—where he would catch you when you tumbled off the earth. He would hold you. He was waiting—

I could see up the evangelist's crow-black nose. Where else was there to look? Up the hem of his whip-stitched coat sleeve?

> And there shall be a tabernacle
> for a shade from the heat
>   and for a place of refuge, and for
>   a covert from the rain.
> *Isaiah 4:6*

The evangelist said he felt moved to pray for the people. He leaped from the platform, dropped his microphone with a clunk. Someone rushed to hand it back to him while we kept our hands to our ears.

"The mind of Christ is our escape from human

limitation." He shouted. "If we're ourselves, we miss the spirit. We live diminished."

"Amen." Nealy beside me said.

"What's your problem, sister?" The evangelist stood by my shoulder.

"My sister has a cough. I'm afraid she's got bronchitis." He held his microphone to my mouth.

"Pneumonia." I heard mother say.

The evangelist prayed for Nealy. Bill looked agitated.

"What's your need, sister?" He asked me.

"Headache."

He jerked me from my chair. My head suddenly pounded like Gus banging his head. My arms raked the wall.

"Leave her alone," I heard Bill.

The evangelist's voice tore into me. When he prayed, his prayers seemed like birds wearing red dresses they changed for blue ones, then purple, murrey, cranberry, newspaper print and finally ink.

"Move on," I heard Bill tell the evangelist, which amplified over the evangelist's loud-speaker.

The gospel choir stopped humming. The ministers on the platform stopped praying. Bill pushed the evangelist from me. But it was the closing of the

Chronicle he pushed against, and the frustration that hedged him.

Mother was in her height of ecstasy. There was the possibility of a fist fight at the revival.

The ministers jumped from the platform. Now there was noise and more confusion.

Didn't even the spirits wrestle against darkness? Weren't we just a copy of the heavenly realm? Lighted by the high-beam of Farley's camera.

What's wrong with these people? Nealy and I ducked by our chairs as Bill shoved at the ministers who tried to stop him. Was nothing ever right? Were we wild to the core? Was darkness always in us? All my days returned. Mother yelling at Bill. The gulping of Farley's fish on our porch.

Overhead I imagined airplanes. Their searchlights on the armory. On the whole earth in fact as they fought holy fires and wars. The plane-lights and camera flashes. The worlds of war and famine and pestilence and death. Pollution. And stupid humanity. The gravel in the tread of our tennis shoes. Were we all lost? Was anything sane in the holy city of Christianity on this earth?

Was it just a brush fire burning windbreaks leaving us open to the elements being dust we would recog-

*nize our pitiful state and accept Christ and be jerked out
of this poke-town small backwater where waves ate us
and what was left was served on plates to our parents to
take apart the rest with their teeth and I was petrified I
would do the same to my children and lived far down in
the basement of myself and would not let it out.*

*In the pounding of my head Christ put his foot on
the neck of that fear and broke it until it was paralyzed
never to rise but waiting my redemption after death
when it would be jerked out at the end of the long tunnel.*

I stood up from under my chair. The ushers
were nearly finished holding people back. The ministers who had leaped from the stage to the floor of
the armory were restoring order. Setting the evangelist upright who then heard my words.

"MY HEADACHE'S GONE!" I wanted to
give my testimony.

"Say it louder." The *brouhaha* seemed hushed a
moment. The evangelist held his microphone to his
swollen mouth. The ushers still wrestled Bill to the
floor. Nealy and Pastor Hill was down there also
praying for him. Others were trying to quiet mother.

"GONE!" I shouted.

The bleeding evangelist suddenly remembered
where he was—he held his handkerchief to his

mouth. "What's your name, sister?" the evangelist asked.

"Hadley."

He pulled me to the stage through the fallen spirits on the floor, the black spirits looking for a flock of pigs to jump into and run them over the cliff into the sea.

"Tell the folks what happened, Hadley," the evangelist said as the battered were restored. I saw the men ushering Bill to the door followed by mother, Nealy and Pastor Hill. Others were trying to upright their chairs so they could see. "My headache's gone."

"GONE!!" The evangelist roared. "GONE!" he screamed to the unbelievers.

A shout went up in the church. The gospel singers hummed. "WOOOOHH!"

"We crossed over the high-link fence of heaven," the evangelist said. The church went wild. The evangelist hipped. The ministers jumped. The people praised the living God. Somewhere out back I still could hear the clatter of mother's voice and the click of Farley's camera.

Fever

"We nearly had a blow-out," I said to Thomas as we came into the house after the revival.

"Bill's in the kitchen," Thomas said. "I know."

I had invited some of the ministers to my house after the revival. Dad had left the armory in a huff. I needed a ride anyway.

I went to the kitchen and started coffee. Hertess and Winifred cut the cake they had made. Jennifer helped them.

"Juan Piccola couldn't have done better," I said to dad.

"We always fear lack of gasoline and water when we travel." Nealy was talking about Africa when I returned to the living room.

"Africa's in turmoil." I heard a man named Fornoy ask about a province where he knew a missionary.

"That's in the south," she said. "I'm west, and to the north." They talked politics awhile. In traveling, the town came up quickly. The huts. The wide flat plain of Africa. The simmering land crackled in the fireplace as Nealy talked. The light from the fireplace jumped along the family pictures on the wall.

"I remember," Pastor Hill said to my dad, who had joined us in the living room, "back when newspapers published what the preachers said on Sunday."

Dad laughed.

Jennifer sat with Winifred as Hertess talked about history. It looked like Farley wasn't going to show up. I even heard mother laugh. Slowly the evening tamed.

Heat and cold, damp and dry, *by thee have I run through a troop, and by my God, have I leaped over a wall*—Psalm 18.

Mother and dad left after a while. Thomas brought more wood into the fire. Pastor Hill remembered the old days, how the Lord had been with him always. Pastor Reams talked about those converted at the revival, of those whom the Lord had convicted of their need to be saved and of those who had laid their burdens on the altar.

Edward Macs and his wife were talking to the man named Fornoy.

"We come rejoicing," I heard Pastor Hill's voice again.

Winifred and Hertess turned their attention to

Pastor Hill. It was going to snow. They'd better get started back to Hammergies. Thomas asked them to stay the night and leave early in the morning. But Pastor Hill wanted to get back. The new highway was straight and they could travel late. Pastor Hill wanted to get ready for his sermon in the morning.

"But those are the Levitical offerings in our lives," Pastor Reams was saying to Nealy as I took the coffee cups and plates into the kitchen. I saw Thom go upstairs. "David admitted his failures and justified God," Pastor Reams said.

Others were leaving as I listened to Pastor Reams. Thomas helped them with their coats. Jennifer had gone to sleep in a corner of the sofa.

"Then the Lord begins to work that evenness of his character within us. That's the meal offering." Reams continued. "We let him grind our rough grains into flour."

"And the burnt offering?" someone asked, ready to leave.

"It's Christ devoted to God. David did what God wanted him to, while Saul did what Saul wanted to."

"But Leviticus begins with the burnt offering," Nealy said, "and you have it last."

"In Leviticus, the offerings are from the center of God outward to man. We begin where we are, at our trespasses, and go toward the fellowship of God in the burnt offering."

The Fuller's Field

"You know what happened," I said as the fire burned low and everyone had gone but Pastor Reams and his wife. "Tonight I felt your angels, Nealy. They were flapping their wings. I felt them over me—I felt them inside my head—a whirlwind of angels cleaning out—I've never left a dish of seed for them on the windowsill in winter like you did, Nealy, but they were there. Once I felt like the circus lady shot from her cannon— Did you ever feel that way, Nealy?"

"No— You were always there with me," she said, "and Gus was the point-man. He was out there first. As long as I could hear his engine noise I knew we were alive."

*　　*　　*

Rough times. Biscuits. Self-will and sorrow, print-potholders and semé smocks in Aunt Mary's kitchen, plowed up windbreaks. The Lord has his way in the whirlwind and in the storm—as I followed his dustcloud down the long road—and the clouds are the dust of his feet—Nahum 1:3.

Snow

Nealy sat in the chair in my living room when I dimmed the lamp after the Reamses had gone.

"I'll go to the church without sleep," she said. "I want to stay up with the snow. You can go to bed, Hadley," she told me.

"I'd rather stay with you."

The snow fell under the street light. As the fire went out, we felt the cold sift into the room. Nealy sat in the chair, her knees drawn up to her chest. She was concentrating on the snow.

A car went by the house, muffled by the snow, yet with the whirr of its tire-chains.

I shivered feeling the loneliness of God in the universe and took the cream pitcher to the kitchen.

"It comes, Nealy—" I said returning from the

refrigerator. "I had nothing, and now I have something. It keeps running— Nealy, remember the water trough?"

"There's nothing he can't fill," she said.

"Except our rejection of him," I answered.

"When I'm in Africa, I think of the feedstore in Hammergies, Hadley. The sacks of barley on a damp, hot day. The grain dust in the air."

"The feedstore had understanding, Nealy, didn't it?"

"I never knew you saw it that way too," she said. "I always thought I missed things you saw."

"I always thought it was I who missed what you and Aunt Mary saw."

Gunnysacks, rafters, pinto brown and mauve prints, the Cornwallis.

We looked at the holy, falling snow.

"Abraham waited twenty-five years for the promised son," Nealy said and I stood at the window with her.

Clearing the Fireplace

The family was the dirty fireplace, I thought as I shoveled ashes in the hard morning light. I could hear the birds through the tunnel of the sky, even a plane and the traffic-noises from the street. They sounded small and far away. Yes, Jesus was the *Fuller Man* who held us together, who shoveled the ashes of our fire, who kept us from blowing apart. He shredded outer-space. Yes, over the vast waves of teeth.

Farley

I was finishing the revival story at the *Chronicle* when Bill called. He'd found Farley in his apartment on the floor. He'd had a stroke. I went to the hospital where Farley was near death. Nealy, Bill and Hertha Jollet stood by his bed. Mother sat in the hall. She had called Gus, she said.

"Hold on, Farley," I told him. "The earth's trying to shake you from its back. The box's tipped and you're the last gumdrop stuck in the corner."

We were silent for a while, except Farley's *tuba*

played now and then. I could only talk in pieces. Bill sat with his head in his hands.

"I've made steadiness my camera," Nealy said. "The gospel's my editor. I know the shore is there."

Farley in his bed looked strangely like a picture he had taken. He never opened his eyes to look at us—nor made any attempt to stay—

That night he folded with the *Chronicle*.

The Cornfield

We had Farley's service at The Cornfield. It was crowded with reporters and old friends. I sat between Thom and Jennifer. Thomas, Nealy, Bill and mother were on the other side of Jennifer. Hertha Jollet still played her tuba behind us. Mr. Creveling, Juan Piccola, Margaret Crussel and Gramilla sat with her.

Gus had gone to Hammergies to get his wife and baby, and they came in late. Hertha stopped her noise for a moment and looked at them.

We said what we remembered about Farley.

The service lasted nearly two hours. Reporters were crowded together at tables. Others stood around the room. After everyone had a chance to say what they wanted about Farley, Nealy read a scripture and prayed.

Afterwards, we ate at The Cornfield. Then Thom drove Jennifer back to our house. Gus, his wife and baby followed.

We talked about what to do with Farley's ashes, whether to leave them in Mussel Fork or Flat Creek. Bill decided he would keep them in his study with Farley's cameras and photographs. Maybe when Bill passed on, their ashes could be scattered together, which set mother off on a tirade. I don't know why he hadn't learned through the years. What would he do with her? She asked. Bury her under the mock orange bush while he and Farley went off together?

"What did it matter?" I thought, but mother reviewed her sorrows while Nealy calmed her.

I knew I would never feel her passion. I would never leap a cornfield like Farley. I would not scream though I had reason to. I was smothered by my will for survival.

Farley could hold a river still in his photographs. I would keep it moving. I would give Thom and Jennifer a level shelf to walk. I would drown in ordinariness and stability and boredom before I'd give them what mother had given us.

I listened to the reporters and newspaper people in The Cornfield.

I would hold a steady climb out of the muck. I felt Farley there with his camera, taking the tears I wouldn't let out of my eyes.

Departure

Two Sundays after Farley's funeral, the missionary offering was taken for Nealy. She was returning to Africa. She sat on the front pew of the church with the children. One held his offering basket on his head. Nealy put it back on his lap. Another hit the child next to her with her basket. Nealy took the child on her lap. Soon there was prayer and the children came up the aisles of the church with their baskets outstretched to the rows of people.

"We're in all things made like unto him." I

heard Nealy's sermon after the drip of coins into the collection baskets.

Nealy was faithful like Samuel when there was none faithful around her. I had sat with her in churches all our lives like birds on the telephone wires. I had passed through the fuller's field following her.

Nealy's voice grew stringy as she talked of Africa and her time there. I sat on the edge of the pew. It was as if Aunt Mary spoke from the pulpit. What she'd always wanted to do. I heard the old tabernacle curtain rip in her voice. She had broken through.

The Take-off

I could see Nealy flying over the ocean. Her eye like a chickenhawk perusing the barnyard.

She looks into the ocean as if the U-shaped wheel were in her hand. It must look something like the steering column on Grandpa Corder's tractor.

At night the sky hangs over her with its wings. Or maybe the universe waves palm branches for the lonely missions it gives. Above her, the stars as instrument panels shine from their fields.

Maybe bugs will buzz like propellers—or a farm pond will shine like a wadi.

Prairie Grass

Bluejoint and saffron.

Farley's cameras had been his wife and children. His trough never seemed to run dry. I looked through his pictures as Bill and Nealy and I cleaned out his files at the *Chronicle*. I showed Bill his photographs of old gravestones. He had taken a picture of a woman before her husband's grave, and the shadow from a massive stone beside her made a black shape in the picture as though a slanted doorway from the unknown had opened for her also.

"Moly-Moly," Bill said.

"Even the grave opened for Farley and his cameras."

Farley's photography was his religion and ministry. He took pictures of his ideas.

"I think sometimes he already saw what he

shot. He only waited for the objects to align with his vision."

"Farley's got an eye—" I'd heard the editor say more than once. Sometimes I thought our words were in the paper to accompany Farley's photography.

"No, his photos were in relationship to our words," Bill said. "He used our copy to form the tension between them."

"But how about the photos he took before the articles were written? Look how he could sustain, yet demolish," I said. "We should collect his photos in a book. His camera was his tabernacle."

Rapture

After Nealy returned to Africa, I thought I heard her in the night. I listened in the room. She was by herself where she walked. In the dim light from the window, I saw wet spots on the floor as if water could run through her feet.

I could see her image. She wore feedsack wings. Something dripped from the ceiling— Was she up

there? Was she tramping around—looking for Farley?

"Nealy?" I said.

There's grape preserves, Hadley, she called, *and
no headaches—* We can walk on water. *—Christ
cannot drown. We walk with him and he holds us up.*

But the cannibals—I said to her—

*—He has on a fish suit with scales that teeth
cannot hurt.*

COLOPHON

Diane Glancy is the author of several novels including *The Only Piece of Furniture in the House* and *Flutie*. She has won numerous awards including the first North American Indian Prose Award and the Capricorn Prize for poetry. Part Cherokee, Glancy teaches Native American literature and creative writing at Macalester College in St. Paul, Minnesota.

The text was set in Caslon, a typeface designed by William Caslon I (1692-1766). This face designed in 1725 has gone through many incarnations. It was the mainstay of British printers for over one hundrted years and remains very popular today. The version used here is Adobe Caslon. The display faces are Insignia and Staccato 222.

The book was composed by Alabama Book Composition, Deatsville, Alabama and printed on acid free paper by Edwards Brothers, Lillington, North Carolina.